A CHRISTMAS KISS

Cindy Powers has a special gift: sometimes she can see into the past or the future. One such vision shows her a picture of Christmas years before, with someone who was very special to her — before it all went wrong between them. But why is it coming back to haunt her now?

ALAN C. WILLIAMS

◆

A CHRISTMAS KISS

Complete and Unabridged

LINFORD
Leicester

First published in Great Britain in 2023 by
D.C. Thomson & Co. Ltd.
Dundee

First Linford Edition
published 2024
by arrangement with
the author and
D.C. Thomson & Co. Ltd.
Dundee

*A catalogue record for this book is available
from the British Library.*

ISBN 978–1–4448–5423–7

1

We all have memories. Everyone we ever knew. But places have memories, too. Places like Hesketh Park, the gently forested area I was wandering through with my daughter on this chilly day.

Pleasant times and tragedies had been gathered without fear or favour, all woven intricately into the fabric of the trees and earth and stones of the pathways that skirted the lake and fountains.

I loved ambling in this natural oasis, but already I sensed that this December morning was special. Very special, in fact, and not necessarily in a good way.

As we slowed our pace, my eyes searched the surroundings furtively, my heart beating ever so slightly faster. I grasped my daughter's hand tightly, sensing those whispers of bygone times waiting in the subtle winter shadows.

Only those phantom memories weren't hovering on the edge of our reality any longer. They were coming for me. With a silent sigh and the barest breath of decaying vegetation, those yesteryear moments reached out towards me with snaking tendrils of mistletoe and ivy, slowly and inexorably, each one eager to take me in their grasp.

As a child, I walked among this wonderland of natural trees and the lake in the midst of the sprawling streets of Southport with my mother holding my hand. Any season. Any weather.

As we'd entered today, my four-year-old daughter's hand in mine, I realised I'd become my mother. The strawberry blonde hair was the same, the wrinkles hopefully not — at least not for a few years.

Amber was pensive this morning, clutching the bag of duck food in her tiny hands, but she was strangely subdued, too.

Perhaps it was this place, the hushed quiet, the sun barely seen through the patches of mist, the frosty grass crunching as we walked across it leaving a trail of greener grass where we'd stood.

I smiled down at her cherubic face.

'How many more sleeps until Santa comes, sweetie?'

She was smart. She knew the dates from the Advent calendar. Surprisingly, she didn't use her fingers this time.

'Fourteen, Mummy.' Her smile and eyes were barely visible inside the brightly coloured scarf wrapped around her head. My dad gave her that. She loved yellow. It suited her, golden and cheerful. But today it seemed as her smile faded.

'A penny for your thoughts, darling,' I said.

She asked me what a penny was. I began to explain then gave up.

Normally, she understood grown-up talk as there was just the two of us most nights and, rightly or wrongly, I shared my thoughts with her, my joys and my worries. Her dad wasn't on the scene. He never wanted her, then or now.

'What's bothering you, pumpkin?' There. My direct approach would force her to answer.

'I'm worried that Santa might not realise that we live in a different house, Mummy, and he won't find me.'

I should have suspected the reason for her anxiety. Amber still called our apartment a house. We'd been there less than ten weeks. I hated it there, mainly because there was no garden for her to run around and explore.

This park, close by and on the way to drop her off at my parents', was the next best thing and at this early hour, there was no one else around, apart from the ducks.

I promised that we'd write a letter to Santa tonight, telling him her new address. Also, I explained that, because we had no chimney, he'd use magic to enter and leave her presents, lovingly wrapped as only his elves could do. Her eyes lit up.

Amber loved magic and princesses and Barbie, and all the things I loved as a child. The smile returned and my sunshine daughter was back. I envied her the innocence of childhood.

We made our way down the winding path past the first of the lake fountains, stopping to pick up russet and tangerine-coloured leaves that smelt of damp earth from the dappled carpet on the ground.

We had time. And if I were late to the gift shop that I owned with my sister, Georgia, she'd understand.

I'd drop Amber off with Mum and then walk into Southport town. Christmas was a special time for our shop, just like with Amber. For different reasons, though.

The chill of the past swallowed me. The past was always cold whether my vision was that of a scorching summer day or that house fire I witnessed as a ten-year-old girl.

Moreover. it was an empty cold, not steeped with dampness like a British winter. The air was but an echo of what used to be, after all.

Today's visions of the past were just as close yet they had never been so intense. I heard children's laughter this time, smelled the hot, roasted chestnuts being sold in tiny white paper bags at the park entrance, felt the ghostly dog on a lead brush past my leg.

I stopped, spellbound by the presence of a Christmas morn from years ago. I'd been here then and now I was back again.

The feeble sun was peeking through the misty air, the still air was tinged with satsumas and pine and cinnamon, all vying for my attention. Were they from the people walking by, gloved hand in gloved hand, their breathing and banter forming momentary clouds before their faces?

Carollers were there also, the rousing words of 'Good King Wenceslas' drifting to my ears. The lake was frozen though no patches of white snow dappled the paths and grass.

It was the magical day of my first kiss. And I stopped as that memory engulfed me in its frigid embrace.

In the distance, I spied my younger self cuddled up to him as they walked hand in hand like those other lovers, that silly red and green hat with the pom-pom dangling down, the one Granny Powers knitted.

Her cheeks were rosy from the bracing cold, that look of bliss on her youthful face and in her eyes. I waved to get her attention, that smiling, innocent me. She ignored me or didn't notice — I wasn't sure which. Did the past share those glimpses into the future as I peered into the past? Honestly, I had no idea.

Slowly, the image faded as remembrances always did. If I could have warned her, or even said hello and to be strong, but I didn't.

Saddened by my return to our solitary present with just the two of us in the park, I stared down at Amber's face, my breathing rapid but slowing.

My latest close encounter with yesteryear thankfully was a reminiscence once more.

* * *

It wasn't the first time I'd been witness to strange vistas of the days gone by. Some might call it a gift, some a curse. As for me, the jury was still out.

Over the years, I'd had these other worldly experiences maybe fifteen times in different locations around Southport. When Jimmy and I moved, nothing strange occurred. I speculated that my home town had unique properties that allowed these time fluxes.

A fluctuation in the Earth's magnetic field, those magical ley lines that supposedly joined up places of power like Glastonbury and Pendle and Stonehenge might criss-cross here? Whatever the mysterious reason was, it didn't make any difference to me. I wasn't a scientist; merely was a spectator.

As to the special places where time ebbed and flowed like the ocean waves, I called them Elsewhens. Other people referred to them as time-slips. That acclaimed writer, the one who created 'The Sandman' graphic novels, he called them Soft Places. I liked that term, too.

But not many people saw them in the same way that not everyone had a good sense of smell. Evolution, I guessed. Or simply genetics.

Society had many terms for women like me, possessed with the ability to see beyond the here and now. We were often regarded with derision by 'normal' people, afraid of those who were different. Psychics who foresaw the future, those who saw ghosts, spiritual mediums who claimed to commune with those loved ones long since departed and women, like me, who peered into the past through strange windows that opened in reality.

It wasn't a part of my life that I shared with many. Stories of witches being burnt at the stake or drowned tended to mean people in my shoes kept their mouths shut.

Yeah. Places were filled with memories. Especially me and this park. Steeling myself, I breathed deeply and wiped my nose with a woman-sized Kleenex. Time to deal with the here and now — Amber. I ruffled my daughter's curls, much to her annoyance.

The ducks swam towards the shore near us in anticipation of a meal. I wondered if they recognised us, maybe Amber with her mustard yellow scarf. Birds saw colours. I read that years ago.

Amber greeted them, calling them by names as she scattered the morsels. It didn't matter that Daisy was much smaller than yesterday. If Amber believed they were the same then that was fine with me.

Together, we watched as the ducks clamoured around the scattered food, their ungainly waddles and honking making Amber giggle. The larger bird in their midst was more reserved. Neither of us humans noticed the man approaching from behind.

'Looks as though that silly goose didn't get the message about flying south for the winter,' he said, keeping his distance. He had a strange accent — Australian or Kiwi. Looked like the large bird wasn't the only one a long way from where he should be.

I glanced at him. A heavy coat and drab scarf almost covered the bright blue shirt and fawn trousers. His dark brown hair was unkempt and too long. He hadn't shaved, either, designer stubble giving way to a scruffy, short beard. Even with gloves and a pork-pie hat, he was strangely dressed for this time of year.

I nodded towards the ungainly bird.

'That goose is a gander called Guy Fawkes. I think he lost his compass so he decided to stay here until some kind soul offers him a lift in their car. Or maybe he believes he's simply a very tall duck.'

Guy (so named by the locals as he first appeared the day of Bonfire Night) was happy to share the seeds from Amber's now empty paper bag.

The stranger stared at my face, recognising some aspect of me, it seemed.

'That makes sense. Good thing that he's not bothered about this weather. Lucky him. I'm freezing.'

For the first time, I noticed him shivering despite being rugged up so much it was hard to tell if he were slim and muscular or somewhat on the heavy side.

One thing was certain, we were the same age or thereabouts.

He shifted on his feet, clasping his hands around his body in an exaggerated attempt to ward off the chill. Poor chap. Yet if he were so cold, why was he here rather than sitting cosily in a warm room?

I checked my watch.

'Time to go, Amber. Granny will be waiting.'

Our shop, The Love Affair, opened at ten and if it were busy first thing, Georgia would need my help. I'd walk there from my parents' place as I didn't have a car. Didn't have a licence, either, as my ex disapproved in the days when I stupidly let him rule my life.

I took Amber's hand.

'Nice to meet you. Enjoy your day.'

'You, too, both of you. I reckon I'll head off to work myself. Much too cold for me despite being done up like an overweight wombat. Before you go, may

I ask a question — did you used to be Cindy Powers?'

I paused.

'I still am . . .'

He grinned, unwrapping his scarf so I can see his face more.

'We went to school together. Warren Ross? Surely you haven't forgotten, Cindy?'

I was shocked.

'Of course I remember Warren but he was . . .'

'Six inches shorter and much rounder? I was a late developer.'

'Wow. If those bullies could see you now.' Back then, I was virtually Warren's sole friend. Then I remembered what happened to our relationship and I stepped back.

He'd hurt me — badly. What he'd done was the ultimate betrayal of our relationship. Warren had denied it yet I'd not believed him. He returned with his mother to Australia a week after that horrible day and I hadn't seen or heard from him since.

13

I shuddered, stumbling as the strength drained from me momentarily. Gallantly, he stepped forward to steady me. Despite my anger with him for all that he did then, that wasn't the reason for my dizziness. It was this Elsewhen Place.

No way that this was a coincidence. One minute I spied my younger self, kissing Warren and then, mere moments later, he returns from the bottom of the world to reappear in my present-day life.

Something quite momentous was happening with us; karma or serendipity or just plain luck weren't enough. Elsewhen was conspiring to reunite Warren and me and it wasn't taking no for an answer.

2

Regaining my balance, I gently extricated myself from his half-embrace with a polite yet reserved thanks. I'd recalled what occurred ten years before and he had no choice than to accept my wish to distance the two of us. Warren wasn't ready to give up, though. He chose a different tack.

'And who's this lovely young lady, Cindy? Your daughter, I presume.'

Amber had been unusually quiet, watching my reactions to gauge what was happening.

I knelt to cuddle her and reassure her that there was nothing to fear from this stranger and that my weakness moment wasn't a concern.

'Amber. This is Mr Ross. Say hello. He . . . he used to be my friend.' Whether I emphasised the 'used to be' or not, Warren ignored my tone.

He knelt, too, extending his hand in

an adult way. Tentatively, she took it and let him shake it gently.

'Hello, Amber. You can call me Warren. Like the holes where bunny rabbits live.' He gave a gentle laugh as she relaxed.

'I like bunny rabbits.' She did a little hop. Warren clapped.

Standing, he faced me.

'I thought you were married and had moved away, Cindy? I never expected you to be here, in our special place.'

I disregarded the last four words. He was mulling over that first kiss, as well. Nevertheless, this park wasn't 'our place' any longer. What was he doing back in Southport? I wanted to ask him but I didn't have the time. Besides, it wasn't as though we'd parted amicably.

'Yeah, I married Jimmy Nolan. You remember him? It didn't work out so well and I moved back here. Listen, Warren. I'd love to chat but I'm in kind of a rush.'

'Just a few minutes, Cindy. You owe me that, for old times' sake.' His eyes narrowed and his deep voice was firm.

I wanted to tell him that I owed him nothing but he was right. We'd left too many things unsaid. Besides, I was curious.

'We can sit on the bench,' he continued, eager not to let me go.

The seat was damp. I hesitated. Warren realised the problem and removed a cloth from his overcoat pocket. My knight in his oversized coat hadn't changed. Always prepared.

Once finished, he stuffed the sodden cloth back in his pocket without hesitation before beckoning me and Amber to sit.

I did, yet Amber chose to return to watching the ducks, staying well back from the mirrored waters of the lake.

Warren joined me, keeping his distance because I placed my bag between us. We began to speak together before he suggested that I start.

Finally, I admitted that I was glad to see him and that he'd changed for the better, at least physically. Being the smallest boy in our senior year had caused him so much anguish. Most girls were taller than him.

He thanked me. That quiet yet intelligent boy whom I'd befriended was still polite and tender. Like me, he watched Amber, ready to react if there was any concern for her safety. I appreciated that.

'Why are you back here — in Southport?' I asked Warren.

'Work. I've been seconded from my job in Sydney. A year over here, based in Liverpool. I'm staying with my grandparents again. Do you still see them?'

I shook my head, feeling guilty about what had happened. We'd fallen out of touch after Warren and his mother returned to Sydney but before that, I'd been a regular visitor to the house on Norwood Road where they all lived.

'The trouble is,' he continued, 'I arrived two days ago. Jet lag plus the change of temperature has taken its toll.' He sniffled.

'It was thirty-plus when I left and my body clock is still adjusting to the eleven-hour time shift backwards. I'd forgotten how miserable your Pommie weather is at this time of year.'

'And yet you're out here in our park, freezing your cute nose off.' I bit my lip. It wasn't appropriate to say 'cute' as I once had. We were adults now and besides, I hadn't forgiven him.

'I reckon the cold's frozen my brain. You're right. Being here makes no sense. I suppose I came to relive pleasant memories. Christmas and this place. Remember?'

I smiled despite my apprehensions.

'Our first kiss? How could I forget that, Warren?' When I said our, it was my first proper one with any boy and his with a girl. At least that's what he claimed back then. Recalling how he was, I had no reason to doubt it.

Not that we were in love or anything. It was a silly teenage dare, an experiment when we were . . . what? Fifteen? It was awkward and fumbling. Our noses kept hitting but eventually, we managed it, pressing our lips together and then drawing back, a little self-conscious. Friends didn't kiss on the lips. Lovers did. Yet that Christmas kiss was wonderful in so many ways.

'You're blushing, Cindy.'

'The cold,' I lied, turning my face to the side. I was suddenly aware of his aftershave. Jovan Musk. He hadn't changed that, at least. Not that he needed it back then as he didn't use a razor.

Amber's eyes watched our non-verbal exchange. It seemed that we were more interesting than the birds at her feet.

'Listen, Warren. We really must get going. My sister will be wondering where I am.'

'Ring her. Here. Use my phone.' He proffered it but I refused politely. I didn't want to touch it or his hand. The hurt was still there. Instead, I stood, calling to Amber. She ran across to me.

Warren stood too, more out of courtesy than anything else. He didn't want us to leave. Perhaps he desired to make things right between us after all these years. Or possibly he simply wanted to talk to a former friend.

'Will I see you again, Cindy?' His voice

had altered from the last time we spoke. It was deeper, seductively smooth like warm, dark chocolate swirling slowly in a cup enticing me to take a sip. I straightened up, facing him.

It was a telling moment. If he were staying nearby then chances were that our paths would cross, especially as it was obvious that Amber and I lived close as well. Also, I'd told him of the shop. It was better to dissuade him at this moment.

'I don't believe it's a good idea, Warren. I'm not in the romance market. Amber's my life now.'

He grinned enigmatically.

'I never mentioned romance, Lucinda Powers. For all you know, I might be happily wed with two kiddies.'

Stupid, stupid, Cindy.

'Nice to see you, Warren. Take care.' I started to walk down the lakeside path towards the Park Crescent exit.

Unfortunately, my curiosity was too strong, so I stopped and called back to him as he wandered off in the opposite direction.

'Warren. Please tell me. Are you married?'

He turned and doffed that ridiculous hat.

'Lovely to see you, Cindy. And you, too, Amber. Till we meet again.' Then he left us, singing 'Jingle Bells'.

I stood there, fuming. That man! Still so aggravating after all this time.

I decided to keep quiet about the chance meeting. Cindy Powers wasn't the brightest girl when it came to relationships. I'd been manipulated by my ex for years into believing he loved me and now Warren had half-convinced me that he wasn't responsible for his betrayal of me back in school.

If Mum found out that we had met, I was sure that I'd have to listen to yet another lecture relating to my questionable choice of men. We were slowly rebuilding our relationship after marrying a man she disapproved of.

The trouble was that I'd forgotten about my daughter and her love of telling her nana everything.

3

'How could you be so silly, Lucinda? Honestly! After what Warren did back then? He almost ruined your final year at school.'

I became defensive. My mum and I had a wonderful relationship. She adored Amber but there was a blind spot when it came to my choice of men in my life. She was simply trying to protect me but I wasn't a child any longer.

I'd made my share of mistakes, especially with Jimmy and his sweet-talking ways, yet these days I was old enough to make my own decisions and accept any consequences.

'Mum, just leave it, please. I need to get to the shop.'

We'd made sure that Amber was well out of earshot. She was contentedly watching cartoons whilst playing with Mr Fluff, Mum's Persian cat.

I couldn't blame her for telling Mum

about the man in the park who spoke funny. It was news and she loved to share gossip, emulating my dear mother more than me. Perhaps it wasn't wise to mention the Christmas kiss with Warren in front of her but how was I to know she'd tell my mother all that she saw and heard? It was as though my sweet daughter was a living camera, replaying everything she heard without a pause, fast-forward or mute button.

In the few short moments that I'd taken rubbish bags to the bins, my mother explained that Amber had innocently shared our meeting in glorious Technicolor. I sighed and forced a weak smile, in spite of the anxious moments she sometimes caused.

Little Miss Amber even mentioned my blushing cheeks, not understanding the implications of that revelation. One day soon, I'd have to tell her the meaning of discretion and keeping secrets.

Mum and I made our peace and I hurried off to The Love Affair. I would be a few minutes late for the ten o'clock opening but, as Mum reminded me, Georgia wouldn't be alone. Our assistant, Hannah, was finished at her private school for the year and was rostered on today.

I'd completely forgotten that. Warren's appearance had addled my brain far more than I believed.

* * *

With just two weeks until Christmas, I took my time to appreciate the festive decorations and atmosphere in my home town during the walk along Lord Street. The conical Christmas trees on the roundabout were resplendent with twinkling decorative lights.

Many of the shops were alive with seasonal window displays. There was even a street vendor selling hot chestnuts. The distinctive smoky odour, as I passed by, took me back to younger, more pleasant times. For a fleeting moment, I wondered if that same vendor was there eleven years earlier, outside the park.

When I reached the front of our shop on the pedestrian precinct, I paused to make certain that the special display was in order. Georgia had a rare talent for the arrangement of our gifts, enticing window shoppers to stop and feel good, hopefully, to step inside for an impulse buy.

At the shop, it took me a good fifteen minutes and a welcome mug of hot chocolate before I defrosted. I thought back to Warren's temperature dilemma; thirty degrees to zero in a few days.

I wondered what his job was that he was able to relocate for a while. Sales rep for some huge international company, or maybe a model? He'd certainly changed from the boy I once went to school with.

During a lull of Christmas gift seeking customers, I had a word with my younger sister about this morning's encounter. As expected, she sided with Mum.

'Did he at least apologise for the malicious leaflets?'

'Not really. He still denies it. Perhaps we got it wrong and it was another student? I mean, him doing that to me was totally out of character.' I was defending him now but back then I was in bits.

I overreacted big time at the ordinary photos of me captioned with cruel words. My few other friends stepped forward at the time to offer solace but it wasn't enough. What a drama queen I was, with no inkling of just what real anguish was in store for me.

Mum and Georgia had to deal with my anger, shame and bucket loads of tears. Dad, too. It ruined my self-confidence so that I was easy prey for that snake, Jimmy, to move into my shattered life.

Unlike Mum, my sister didn't go on and on regarding me meeting Warren. I appreciated that and told her so. She'd gone to university, met her lovely husband and suggested this joint venture of opening The Love Affair when I returned from Preston, newly divorced with Amber by my side. My daughter was the one good thing from my marriage and I silently thanked Jimmy for that.

Whether it was an olive branch to repair the damage caused by my marriage and all those family fights was immaterial. Georgia gave me a sense of purpose again, and self-worth.

I used the profit from my half of the house sale to help with the shop lease, refitting and stock. It was pointless to buy again until I had a definite plan for the future. Renting our two-bed apartment close to the park and town made sense. I loved Southport and should never have left but Jimmy convinced me to and like the fool I was then, I didn't object.

At least he was out of mine and Amber's life for good.

Yet all through the day, my mind kept returning to that memory of a shivering Warren in the park. Was Mum right about my naivety? Was I already becoming fixated on another man, if solely to boost my self-esteem? And if so, why Warren? That daft, childish kiss?

I'd heard enough stories concerning love on the rebound but that wasn't for me. I was a mother first and foremost.

The last thing I desired was another man in my life.

We had a steady stream of customers most of the day, even after it grew dark around four pm. Our shop was fortunate to have the support of both locals and visiting tourists alike. In a world where town centre shops were closing every day, Southport people were keen to support new ventures, especially those offering unusual items.

Personally, I believed in the dream of having a special item to touch rather than buying it from the internet. The experience of choosing from the shelves should be a joyful part of the purchasing process.

The Love Affair offered our clients the opportunity to lose themselves in atmospheric worlds where unique modern gifts shared the space with selected antiques and collectables. The display cabinets and velvet or silk-adorned shelves were complemented with evocative lighting.

It was coming up to five-thirty — closing time. More people entered, browsing rather than rushing. I returned to the service desk as young Hannah was busy gift-wrapping a Victorian tea set.

Georgia was busy with paperwork in the small kitchenette but came out, clearly agitated. We waited until the last shoppers left, then closed the shop. I sensed her eagerness to share whatever news she had. From the expression on her face, it wasn't good.

'What's up?' I asked. Hannah was eager to hear, too.

'You remember Bart Travis, don't you, Cindy? Wasn't he in your year at school?' So was Warren, but I pushed thoughts of him to one side to concentrate on this revelation. Georgia showed us her phone, opened on the local Facebook page. They were first with any news, being aligned with the local station, Mighty Radio.

We took turns reading the article. Bart was the son of one of the local business owners and his family was always on the social pages as they donated to the charities in the area. I gasped.

Bartholomew (he hated being called that)Travis had been abducted and a ransom was being demanded, although no figure had been mentioned.

'I can't believe it. A kidnapping here in Southport?'

Hannah read the post.

'It says that your dad's in charge of the investigation.'

Well, that made sense. He'd been a Detective Chief Inspector for years.

'Listen to this: 'The young executive was snatched whilst on an early morning jog along the dunes near Ainsdale yesterday morning. His phone was found in the sands when the phone was traced once he was reported missing'.'

We all fell silent before she Georgia spoke.

'Mike and I have met the family a few times at various events. They must be so anxious. But at least Dad's on the job.'

It was my turn to ask questions.

'Yet if this happened yesterday and he found out then, why not say anything to Mum or you?'

31

Georgia didn't have an answer to that. Perhaps the kidnappers had insisted on discretion around the incident, yet someone had leaked the story today. It was useless to speculate.

Finally, I asked her how Dad would cope with being SIO (Senior Investigating Officer) on another abduction case, recalling how badly the last one ended. The ransom was paid but when the location of the victim was investigated, he was dead. The post-mortem confirmed that it was down to a lack of his medication rather than any violence.

However, his death, even if by accident, was tragic and the police team involved shared the anguish of the young man's family at his loss.

'We always suspected that Dad's mind was distracted from the abduction although he'd never admit it, Cindy. The school situation was at the same time, the one where you were in pieces over the posters that Warren plastered all over the school about you.'

'What?'

'You were a real mess back then, Cindy. Rightly so. The things he wrote mentioning you were awful and the public humiliation was simply criminal. Mum and I tried but you were so emotional, yelling at us and refusing to show our face in public or return for the exams.

'Dad had the kidnapping thing on his plate. It was the same week. He was the one who found that Warren was responsible for those lies, typing them out on a school computer. Nevertheless, he was distracted from a much worse crime which ultimately led to a man's death.'

I began to cry. Back then I'd been so selfish. I remembered yelling at my father, begging him to find out the name of the person who ruined my reputation because he was a copper. And because he loved me, he had. But at what cost?

He tracked down the instigator for me, upsetting me more as it was my friend, Warren, who'd spread the lies. Meanwhile, that abducted man was dying because he didn't have his medication to keep him alive and the kidnappers didn't appreciate how ill he was. If Dad hadn't been preoccupied with my drama-queen crisis, would that man still be alive? I'd never know.

'Georgia,' I said, at last, dabbing a soggy tissue to my eyes. 'What was his name? The kidnap victim back then?'

To my shame, I'd forgotten it, as I had many of the things from those weeks. Someone said that it was a survival mechanism to force hurtful times to the back of my mind. I guessed that meant most things from that period.

'William Lockstone. He was twenty-two, a diabetic. Dad still visits the parents from time to time.'

I remembered the name once she said it, along with the heartfelt pleas his family made on the local telly for his safe return.

I was far too aware that bullying was more insidious these days with social media and texting destroying the self-confidence of far too many girls and boys. A whispered innuendo, a confidence stupidly shared with a close friend then being circulated to everyone to cause maximum hurt.

Not that I'd thought of anything too drastic back then. Dad exposing Warren as the person who instigated those hurtful words relating to me had helped mitigate the harm he did. He left our school and my life for Australia soon afterwards, always protesting his innocence.

Yet today, Warren was back and there was another kidnapping. Surely there couldn't be a connection, could there? I asked Georgia who dismissed the idea immediately.

'Heavens above, Cindy. I'm not your Aussie mate's greatest fan but you told me he just arrived in England. No-one — and I mean no-one — arrives with jet lag one day and immediately snatches a guy out running for ransom. It's just a coincidence.' She checked the time on her watch.

'Ladies? Can we lock up and get going? And tomorrow I don't want to hear you mention Warren. Please?'

I nodded. She was right. Best to put him out of my mind. If he just arrived there was no way he'd be involved in this crime. I felt a wave of relief that lasted until we'd closed the door and gone our separate ways, me to meet Mum and Amber at a nearby café, Georgia to go home to her husband and Hannah to the local choir for carol rehearsals.

Mum had brought Amber into town earlier for shopping and a visit to see Santa. She was off to her book club so we'd arranged for a quick meeting and drinks before I went home with my daughter.

Warren's name wasn't mentioned once, therefore we had a pleasant catch-up, the three of us. Once Mum left, I decided to make use of the warmer cloudy evening to show Amber the special Christmas tree near the Atkinson with its co-ordinated rainbows of lights in every colour dancing before our eyes. She loved it and a friend I saw there kindly snapped a load of photos of us near the tree.

It had been a memorable day for my little girl, but she was tired. We waited at the bus stop with a few others to catch the bus home. All the trees on Lord Street were lit throughout the year with thousands of white lights. They added to the magical atmosphere.

Once settled on the warm bus, I took out the photo Mum had given me. It was Amber with Santa Claus.

'What did you say to Santa, kitten?'

She smiled back after staring at the precious picture taken by one of Santa's helpers.

'I told him that we moved house just in case he doesn't get our letter in time but he already knewed that, Mummy. He remembered my name and everything. Then he asked me what I wanted for Christmas so I said a Supergirl doll.'

She loved the superhero cartoons.

We were at a bus stop at the end of Lord Street when Amber started waving excitedly.

'Look, Mummy. There's Grandpa.'

Considering that the police station was

on the other side of the roundabout, she was probably right. I peered through the window. Yeah. There was Dad, all right, shaking hands with another man before waving goodbye as they went their separate ways.

The bus began moving but I sat there staring.

'What's the matter, Mummy?' Amber asked, again sensing my discomfort.

'Nothing, kitten. A headache . . . that's all.'

Amber was satisfied with my white lie. Or maybe it wasn't a lie as my mind was doing somersaults, trying to make sense of whom I'd seen with Dad.

As far as I knew, he disliked this guy passionately. Certainly, he was the one person whom I'd witnessed my father losing his temper with. Considering that Dad had never shown genuine anger to my unfaithful ex, despite the years of antagonism between them, I was amazed that he was with the fellow I'd seen.

'My father and Warren Ross? What in heaven's name is going on?' I whispered to myself. Tomorrow, I'd quiz my father since I didn't feel up to phoning him later.

One thing was certain — my chance meeting with Warren this morning wasn't going to be a one-off after all.

4

Devina Basu was a twenty-two-year-old stunning beauty in the final year of her degree in psychology in Liverpool. She lived alone downstairs, in our apartment block. We'd been close friends ever since Amber and I moved in.

In this modern world, it's unusual for a stranger to turn up unannounced bearing a plateful of Indian delicacies to welcome us to the block. That she also had a bottle of a fine New Zealand white in her hand had nothing to do with me inviting her in . . .

She was funny and lively and so kind to Amber and me. Amber loved her dearly and always pleaded to hear one of the fairy tales from India that Devina's mother had told her. She loved to cook, too.

Considering that it ranked with ironing as my worst ever job, we quickly came up with one of those win-win situations;

I'd buy the ingredients and Devina and I would prepare the meal together in our kitchen. I was a great gofer whilst Devina did the messy work. Amber tried to help, too.

It was beneficial to Devina as she was a struggling student. Her uncle paid for the flat, rates and utilities and she had some money but never enough. Nonetheless, there was one aspect of my friend that puzzled me. Although she listened patiently to my boring lifetime dramas and stories of my ex and my family, she was strangely quiet about her own family.

Her parents were alive and lived in London but she never spoke of her upbringing or visited them. I sensed that beneath her sparkling personality, bad things had happened to her and she preferred not to share them with anyone. Even me.

'Tell me all about this Warren guy, Cindy.'

We were on to our second glass of Jammy Red Roo.

'Back at school, he was a loner. Maybe that's what attracted me to him. I was always a sucker for an underdog. The others made fun of his accent and physical appearance. Well, more ignored him, I guess. He was shy, too. When he did say something in a group, it was totally wrong . . . inappropriate or just plain dumb.'

Devina sipped her drink, curled up in the armchair whilst I stretched out lazily on the matching settee. They were the only pieces of furniture I'd brought with me after Jimmy and I sold our home.

'And yet you were mates — or more?'

I giggled.

'We were never romantically involved although I always suspected that he fancied me. That first kiss was my idea. I'd seen Bree, my cousin, doing it and curiosity made me wonder.

'And then, in the park, I saw mistletoe hanging from a bare tree. It was one of those moments when it seemed right.'

I checked the monitor set up in Amber's bedroom. She was fast asleep after Devina had told her the story of the Geese and the Tortoise. The moral of the tale when the tortoise died despite efforts by the geese to save him, was that we cannot alter fate.

That made me consider this morning. Was I destined to meet Warren there in the park where we kissed? And if not today, would we have met another day? Also, there was the Elsewhen phenomenon. It was the first occasion that I'd seen myself from another time.

Experiencing the scene through all of my senses was petrifying. In those other instances that I'd witnessed, I was a spectator from afar. Today, I was there . . . an unwilling participant in this otherworldly hole in time.

Had my younger self noticed me and Amber? I tried to recollect but couldn't. My youthful mind was elsewhere.

'Mistletoe, eh? I can never understand that particular tradition. I mean, it's a parasitic plant, feeding off trees, for goodness' sake, Cindy. Hardly an auspicious start to a romantic relationship.'

I'd never considered that.

'Talking of parasites, that sums up Jimmy big-time. All those years subtly feeding on my self-esteem and independence, sucking my very life from me.'

Devina must have noticed the change in my disposition as she stood and gave me a comforting hug.

'Come on, Cindy. Stop dwelling on Jimmy and think of happier things. Perhaps this Warren guy? You never forget your first kiss and all that?'

I managed a sort-of smile.

'Warren? As if. He hurt me, too. Why do I always choose men who betray me?'

Again, a warm hug, this time lasting longer.

'My dearest Cindy. You're unlucky, from what you've told me of this Jimmy guy. But you're a brilliant mum to Amber and the shop is going great from all accounts. Plus, you're my bestie.

'I have my issues with men too . . . Well, one man. Yet there are good ones out there. I'm in no hurry and neither are you, I suspect, but someone will come along that will treat you and Amber with respect, dignity and love.'

She moved away to top up our glasses then raised hers.

'A toast. To finding two perfect men; one for each of us.'

'To perfect men,' I agreed, with a giggle. 'And other fairy tales.' We touched glasses and drank. At least there was no rush to get up early tomorrow although I'd have to deal with the inevitable hangover.

★ ★ ★

I dreamed of that Christmas kiss, for some reason. Mum told me once that dreams were away of processing the events of the day, often revisiting them in a surreal world that was anything but logical.

Although it was ten years ago, that day was clear in every detail. My sister, Georgia, was on a skiing trip to France. Warren's family and mine had chosen to share a meal. Mum worked with Warren's mother and Dad's golfing partner was Warren's grandfather.

With the two mums and Warren's gran busy in the kitchen and the two men watching some football match, Warren and I were told to make ourselves scarce for an hour or two.

The trouble was, nowhere was open. Wandering down to the Promenade and Marine Lake wasn't on the cards as the westerly wind from the Irish Sea was bitter and fierce.

I suggested the park as it was just streets away and protected from the weather. We were rugged up against the cold, scarves and all. I was taller than him but neither of us minded. We shared a Galaxy bar as we walked along the deserted streets to the entrance near the traffic lights.

It was frosty, even at one in the afternoon. We were not alone in the park, as many felt that Christmas was the perfect time to commune with nature, even those noisy ducks. He took my gloved hand in his which wasn't unusual. We were friends, after all.

In retrospect, that's what made me think of the kiss suggestion, although I still believe it was more than that. Perhaps, the sight of other couples, snuggled up and sharing the frosty ambience and joy? More likely was the feeling that I wanted more to remember from this day than carols and unwrapping more pairs of socks and dresses that Mum thought were perfect but I hated.

I was growing up, a young woman at last, with romance on my mind. Yet I didn't have a boyfriend. Maybe I was too plain or too particular. The boys that I fancied didn't give me a second glance. Maybe they stayed away as my father was a copper.

Whatever the reason, I wanted to share something intimate with a guy and Warren was the only one there.

At first, he was shocked telling me that it wasn't one of my better ideas.

'Why?' I said, slightly hurt. 'Do I have bad breath? I thought you'd be flattered to be my first.'

'I am flattered, Cindy. Honest. It's

just . . .'

'Just what, Warren?'

'I've never kissed a girl before. Blokes are supposed to be experts and I don't want to disappoint you.'

I misjudged him, badly. We girls weren't the sole ones afraid of doing things that made us look like fools. I took both his hands in mine, drawing him closer.

'Well, that's OK. It'll be the first time for both of us. I promise I won't laugh even if we hate it. No strings, though. It's one kiss, nothing more. I've heard what boys expect after a kiss.'

His face went red. 'Cindy. I'd never do that. I . . . I don't think of you in that way.'

It wasn't the best thing to say but that was Warren all over. He moved us over to a point where he stood on a concrete plinth under a bench so that he was my height.

'Ready?' I said, our faces inches apart and our breaths already becoming more rapid. 'On the count of three . . .'

'Hold on, Cindy. Eyes open or closed?'

'Closed.' At least that's what one of Mum's old magazines advised.

'Right. Closed. Although I'll have to touch you to know where your lips are, I guess.'

That made sense but I was beginning to have second thoughts about the whole idea. It wasn't going the same way as in the movies.

I completed the countdown then felt his warm, minty breath on my face and felt his fingers tenderly playing with my ears. It was so intimate. Our lips touched then he drew back before pressing softly. I opened my eyes to see him staring back. I'd never seen him so happy.

Something changed between us that day. We never spoke of it again, even when Mum asked what we'd done on our wanderings. She suspected, though. Mums always sense their daughter's secrets.

Although Warren's behaviour wasn't overly different, from time to time I'd catch sight of him looking at me for no reason. When caught, he'd turn away as though he was doing something wrong.

And later, when I began dating boys like Jimmy, he'd make excuses, too, whenever I was with them, as if he disapproved of my behaviour with them. We'd grown apart and I hated that.

When asked if he'd found a girlfriend or someone special in his life, he'd mutter some self-deprecating phrase like, 'Who'd have me?' I tried to boost his fragile ego time and time again before giving up. After all, if he didn't feel good about himself so be it.

Then came the day that tore my life apart; the posting of those cruel taunts everywhere at school.

That was the finish of whatever Warren and I once had. But these days, he was back in Southport and in my life, especially if he were mates with Dad.

★ ★ ★

The following day was my day off at the shop. I'd planned to go into Liverpool by bus to pick up a special present I'd ordered for Amber and do some last-minute Christmas shopping in Liverpool One and the Docks.

Mum would look after Amber in my absence. She was happy to make up for those lost years when she hardly saw her. Dad was more awkward with her which was sad but it was an adjustment that I prayed he'd make soon.

It was another thing I despised Jimmy for, the way he had made meeting or talking to my family so hard.

However, I changed my plans . . . deciding to delay the bus trip down south until after I had a heart-to-heart with Dad.

The walk to the police headquarters took a few minutes. The desk sergeant greeted me.

'Long time no see, Cindy. How are you and the little tyke doing? I bet she's dead excited over Christmas.'

'She is, Uncle Gerry. We'll have to catch up properly soon. Any good news regarding Bart's abduction?'

'No. I'd forgotten you knew him from school. A terrible thing when a man can't go jogging around our town. What can I do you for this morning, anyway?'

'Is Dad free at the moment?'

Gerry Hawkins checked on the intercom, saying he was between briefings and press updates. He'd stayed overnight, bunking down in his office on a campbed. That was bad. He wasn't as young as he used to be and I expected he'd be in one of his grumpier moods.

Gerry gave me a visitor badge before ushering me through the security door. My father greeted me in the corridor on the first floor.

'Good to see you, Cindy. I haven't long, though. What's up?'

His features were haggard, his navy suit quite creased and his old paisley tie hanging loosely around his neck. He had a freshly pressed shirt in one hand, ready to change for the press briefing.

Was I doing the right thing, interrupting him like this? After all, it was a repeat of the drama caused ten years ago where he'd been distracted by my demands.

Steeling myself, I faced him.

'Dad. I realise this is not the best time to ask but I have to know. Are you aware that Warren Ross is back in town?'

He seemed ill at ease with that question.

'Yes. Your mother may have mentioned it last night? Why are you asking, Cindy Bear?' His use of his pet name didn't faze me.

'Only that? What about you both meeting in person at six yesterday evening?' I crossed my arms across my chest and shifted my stance to a more aggressive one, staring at him intently.

He couldn't face me.

'I'm sorry, love. You must be mistaken. I haven't seen him in years . . . Not since you were both in school.'

It was a long pause before I answered.

'You're a terrible liar, Dad. Always were. Clearly, you have your reasons yet I'm disappointed that you can't trust me. It doesn't matter. I'm my father's daughter. I'll do my own investigating.

'Thanks for letting me know one thing, though. Something is going on with Warren.

Him being here and meeting you isn't the coincidence that I first thought it was.'

With that, I turned on my heels to leave.

Dad stopped me with a firm and caring hand on my shoulder.

'Please don't judge me too harshly, Cindy Bear. I wanted to keep you in the dark concerning Warren but I suspect it might be too late. Your mother's said too much already on Facebook, telling everyone and their dogs that he's back in town. Suffice it to say that Warren wasn't responsible for that incident at school.'

I twisted around in shock.

'He wasn't? But you had proof at the time. I remember you saying he was the one to blame.'

Dad was sad and repentant.

'Back then, that's what I was convinced of. I was wrong. So wrong. I did him a great disservice then and that's why

I'm begging you. Please don't mention to anyone that you saw us together last night. I don't want to be too dramatic but it's a matter . . .'

'Of life and death?'

His eyes confirmed my dramatic conclusion. I gasped. My father was deadly serious.

'Your secret's safe with me, Dad. I love you. You know that.'

5

Having left the police station, I did catch the bus to Liverpool. The trip afforded me the opportunity to make sense of Dad's revelation about Warren not being the culprit back in my school years.

That he was guilty of designing the wicked leaflets was accepted at the time by the school and my father. The original document had been put together by Warren on a school computer and stored in his personal folder. That's how he was discovered as the instigator.

Given the nature of the offence, the IT technician soon found it hidden away on the school's hard drive. Everyone knew that our personal folders were not private at all yet Warren had seemingly done it at school anyway.

Considering his talents with software programming, it made no sense yet the incriminating evidence was there.

As he was singled out as the perpetrator,

both staff and pupils branded him a cyber bully. Not that I had many mates at school apart from Shania, Keith, Jimmy and Warren (I believed), but there was a mass of sympathy for the way I was treated and humiliated, especially by other girls.

There, but for sheer dumb luck, they might have been in the same boat. Peer pressure was always tenuous and any one of them might have been singled out, too.

At the time, Warren was intending to stay in Southport with his grandparents whilst his mum returned to Australia but that all changed in an instant.

His reputation was trashed and to remain in our school was more than he could take. His protests that he was innocent, a victim of an elaborate frame, rang hollow with everyone, including me.

My doubts regarding his guilt were dismissed by Jimmy and Shania who were incensed by his betrayal. Yeah. The evidence was there, all right. And my policeman father accepted it as gospel.

Yet, sometime in the ensuing years, Dad unearthed the truth. Another person was to blame. He never told me and I understood why. Digging up that part of my past would not have been appreciated. But now, with Warren back on the scene, Dad was intent on vindicating him, at least in my eyes.

If he did suspect the one who framed Warren, he would have said. By the time I'd done my shopping and returned to Southport, I was none the wiser about the true culprit or the reason that Warren and Dad had their secret meeting.

To be honest, my head was crammed chock-a-block with other issues, including Bart's abduction and yesterday's Elsewhen vision. I had to be careful with my mental health after the traumatic events of my separation. That was the problem of being highly strung.

Alighting from the bus on Lord Street, I made my way to the pedestrian precinct where The Love Affair was. It was my Christmas gift sanctuary for Amber, making sure that her festive surprises weren't discovered too early.

Our second-floor accommodation had no hiding places, and even Mum and Dad's house wasn't safe from my curious child's prying eyes.

It was about four-thirty, bracing, breezy and the sort of evening when anyone would be glad to be snuggled up under a blanket, sipping a hot chocolate.

The shopping hub was busy, though; mothers with rugged-up kiddies admiring the spectacle of Christmas lights and decorations adorning the shops and streets. In addition, workers finished up for the day, nipping into Tescos for a readymeal or the post office to post hastily scribbled cards to people on their outdated Christmas card lists.

Our shop was busy, too, a warm wonderland of joy away from the chilly, clear evening's bite. Hannah hastened to help me with the bags of presents as I shouldered open the front door. I was engulfed by a blast of warming air from the blower above, wafting strands of my hair across my face.

She peeked inside her bags as she ushered me to the store room out back.

'Looks like Santa's been very busy, Cindy.'

'She deserves it. She's tolerated too many bad things this year. Besides, no presents from Jimmy. He made that perfectly clear when I left.'

Not that he was ever a father in the caring sense of the term yet to cut himself off totally from her life was a surprise, even to me. It was his feeble but spiteful revenge for our divorce and depriving him of my inheritance.

Far from being the caring man whom I fell in love with, Jimmy confirmed that our entire marriage was a sham with one goal in mind . . . fleecing me of Gran's trust fund.

Conscious of the number of browsers in the store, I promised to show Hannah the toys and clothes after closing. Meanwhile, even though it was my day off, I accompanied her back onto the shop floor, intent on helping our customers choose their perfect special something.

We had a large, child-sized Cupid in the store complete with bow and arrow. The Santa hat was slightly incongruous yet was accepted as a sign of the festive season. He wasn't for sale, more a mascot for our shop's romance theme.

On several occasions since we opened, my sister and Hannah had remarked on me talking to him. Just another indication that I wasn't one hundred per cent normal.

I wasn't alone, though. More than one young lady was spotted whispering to him and touching his alabaster foot. We speculated that Cupid might be Southport's special place to go when prayers for love were sought.

Whatever the reason, he even had his place on our Facebook pages with several postcards displayed on the wall behind, addressed to him from exotic places where sultry, warm breezes blew.

Closing time was almost there when Georgia called me over. I'd informed her about Warren's innocence, at least according to Dad. It was a good thing that I did because the man in question chose to pay a surprise visit to our shop. Otherwise, my defensive sister might have given him a mouthful when he turned up. Because my sister, like me, hadn't recognised him, Warren introduced himself.

'Cindy? There's a talking kangaroo here to speak to you,' she called out.

I came out from the office where Hannah and I were collating the day's sales and unpacking the new stock.

Georgia had her arms crossed with a mock scowl on her pretty face. She'd missed out on inheriting Mum's colouring and had auburn hair with not a freckle in sight.

'I did tell you not to mention his name today, but you're forgiven. However, you should have said how drop-dead-gorgeous he is! If I weren't happily married . . .'

She stopped mid-sentence, conscious of my marital situation. I reassured her that I wasn't that fragile any longer.

Warren stood mutely, grinning slightly

at my sister's totally inappropriate and awkward words about him. Thank goodness there were fewer than a dozen customers, all smiling and admiring Warren's rugged good looks, too.

Six foot two and with one of those bodies that most men might wish was theirs, lean and muscular without being overly so. But it was those blue eyes that captivated me for one blissful moment. Georgia, being Georgia, continued her appraisal.

'I have to admit, Warren. There's no way I'd have recognised you. And what about those dreadful tortoise-shell glasses?'

'Contacts. All the rest is the real me.' His self-conscious laugh reminded me of those last few years in school, him help-ing me with my Maths homework and me simply talking to him.

'Same with Cindy, here. What you see is what you get,' she commented without realising that it might seem that she was offering me up on a plate.

'Well . . . apart from your padded

bra,' she whispered to me, enjoying my embarrassment. I shushed her, uncertain if Warren had heard. He remained politely quiet, glancing away discreetly.

My talkative sister wasn't finished.

'Didn't you go back to Aussieland? A family crisis. But now you're back here. In our shop. What brings you back to windy Southport anyway? Surely not, Cindy?'

He stole a glance in my direction before adopting a quite amenable, nonchalant stance.

'Simply a family visit. My grandparents. Two weeks, possibly three, then back to decent weather. In my humble opinion, snow is great on Christmas cards or for penguins but that's as far as it goes. I hate cold weather.'

I was ready to interject with a question. Hadn't he told Amber and me that he was on exchange for a year? Seeing the enigmatic query in my eyes, he continued before I had a chance to express my concerns.

'As for Cindy and me, I doubt that

she's into one-night or even two-week stands, right? I respect her too much for that.

'Still, I did fancy a proper catch-up . . . purely as mates. A coffee, perhaps? What do you say, Lucy-Lou?'

6

From the tone, I gathered that his polite request was akin to a command. Normally such an attitude would have ended in a defensive rebuke these days. I had my share of Jimmy's treatment over the years and wasn't ready to entertain a repeat of that from any man.

But this wasn't any man. Warren had his reasons and my curiosity was piqued. My nickname from his close friendship was a trigger, too, and he knew it.

I grabbed my bag and camel overcoat, joining him at the door. 'Oi, Aussie. Be gentle with my sister . . . or else,' Georgia called out to him.

'No worries, Georgia. See you again.'

A part of me was pleased with the prospect of a leisurely chat with Warren yet I felt strangely apprehensive.

December was, as always, a fickle month, unsure whether to be simply cool or sometimes downright arctic, especially with a westerly blowing over the Atlantic Ocean. Hit again by the gusty Southport winter, we struggled to put our gloves on.

'Where can you recommend, Cindy?'

I was impressed. He asked my advice rather than assuming that he knew best. Compared to Jimmy, Warren was so much more polite.

'There's a place on Lord Street, a few minutes' walk. The Kaleidoscope. Good atmosphere and I know the owner from my school days. That OK?'

Warren's attire was complemented by an unusual scarf in green and yellow instead of the sombre ones favoured by British men. On anyone else, it might scream football fanatic, on him, it was a simple statement of his antipodean nationality; colours he was proud to wear.

As we entered the restaurant/coffee lounge I noticed the usual lack of people. It was surprising, the more so as it was open with no shortage of staff. These days, for any place to stay trading, that all-important footfall and potential number of covers was crucial, but seemingly not for Keith.

When I returned to Southport, I chose to patronise Keith Giffen's establishment. He supported me during that traumatic time with the leaflets. I owed him. As for The Kaleidoscope, it wasn't everyone's choice of décor. Apart from the child's toy, a cylinder with mirrors and coloured glass, I'd learnt that a kaleidoscope was a collective name for butterflies.

The walls were painted like fields and forests, dappled with cut-out butterflies of every size and colour. Some of them had wings that moved, slow-moving motors secreted to flap their wings. Like I said, an acquired taste. Warren examined the décor and grunted. Not a fan, I gathered.

I asked Alicia, our waitress, if her boss were around. She replied that he was off today.

Our coffee time together began badly. We'd hardly had a chance to order when Warren confessed that our chance meeting in Hesketh Park was a mistake.

'I didn't expect to see you in Southport. It's screwed things up big time, Cindy.'

I wasn't impressed.

'Charming. Are you telling me that our encounter was a mistake, Warren? Because if it is, then I have better things to do than to spend my time listening to you butchering the English language.

'And what was that rubbish about your being here for three weeks? You told me that you were seconded over here for a year. The truth, Mister Skippy, or I walk.'

I made a move to stand until he rested his hand on mine.

'Calm down, Bossy Boots. The truth, eh? You're not going to like it, though. You've changed, Lucy-Lou. I never remembered you being so defensive.' His grin was infectious and I sat again, wary but prepared to listen.

'OK, Warren. But please don't call me, Lucy-Lou. I've grown up. Stupid and naïve Lucy-Lou is dead. You have no idea what my married life was like.'

His expression changed to that of

compassion although he withdrew his open palm from mine.

'Too right. I don't. My grandparents hinted at it and your dad suggested that Jimmy was a control freak but no, I have no idea regarding how you were hurt.

'When I chatted with you in the park, I was so pleased to see you that I didn't think straight. Now, thanks to your mother and her penchant for gossip, I've had to rethink my cover story. Not that I blame your dear mum. She is what she is. I had no idea that you'd share our chance encounter with her.'

'I didn't. Amber did. Takes after her granny, I guess.' I could have taken offence at Warren's description of my mum but I didn't.

She was, in his vernacular, a bit of a stickybeak, delving into anyone's business and then sharing it with the world. Mum had been an avid 'Neighbours' fan, taping every episode. That included a nosy woman called Mrs Mangel from the mid to late Eighties.

Warren and I watched those early

episodes a generation later and both agreed (though never to her face) that Mrs Mangel was Mum's Australian twin sister, separated at birth.

'Sorry. I misjudged you, Cindy. The end result's the same, though. All of Southport knows I'm back which makes my somewhat undercover assignment somewhat redundant.'

My eyes opened wide.

'You're a spy?'

Warren stared at me, aghast.

'No, you fruit loop. I'm a detective on secondment from the New South Wales Police. Why on earth did you think I was a spy?'

'You always wanted to be one. I remember you carried a card saying Secret Agent 005 in your wallet for years. Not the brightest thing for a spy to carry around, in retrospect. How do I know you're a copper?'

Warren retrieved a wallet from his back pocket. He showed it to me quickly before returning it.

'OK. Some things don't change. You

always had an unnatural fixation with cards in wallets. Can I assume that no-one else should find out about this?'

'No-one. Especially your mum. Pinkie promise?'

This time it was my turn to be shocked.

'What are you, Warren? Ten years old?'

He persisted, holding out his bent little finger. He wasn't giving up. Finally, I relented with a sigh and a giggle.

'OK. Pinkie promise,' I agreed as we linked our fingers in a childhood ritual.

Despite the foolishness of it all, I accepted that this immature playfulness was for my benefit. Warren had always known how to drag me from those morose moments in my life back then. He still did, it seemed.

Becoming more serious once more, he slid his chair up near to me, the better to discuss his reason for being back in Southport.

'I was transferred to Liverpool CID, expecting to be working in Liverpool. Then this kidnap comes up. Your dad heard about my arrival and requested me to assist him off the radar. The locals know all the police around here, hence my undercover role.'

We kept our voices low and our faces close. To onlookers, I assumed it looked like a romantic tryst, although the truth was much more intriguing.

'You suspect that Bart was kidnapped by local people?'

'Too right. Also, that his abduction is by the same crew who kidnapped William Lockstone ten years ago. The diabetic who died.'

I was surprised, initially, but upon reflection, it made sense to me. I believed in forces outside our reality — the Else-whens for a start. The two kidnappings, Warren and I being back in Southport at the time of the second, even my vision. Serendipity indeed.

'Funny. I wondered if you were the kid-napper when I first found out, Warren. Also, I had a . . .' I hesitated, deciding not to mention my glimpse of our younger selves kissing. I'd never shared that part of my life with him, afraid that, like too many others, he'd regard me as a liar or a weirdo.

'What were you about to say, Cindy?'

'Nothing. Just trying to make sense of what you're suggesting.'

At that moment, we became aware of a woman pushing the café door open in a hurry. She glanced around, spotted us and ran over, panting, thrusting her mobile phone at us. It was Georgia. She was out of breath.

'Thank the stars I found you,' she gasped as Warren stood to offer her a chair.

'Is it Amber? Mum or Dad? Has something happened to them?'

'No,' she managed to say. Her chest was heaving from running. Normally, she would have rung but I'd forgotten my phone, having left it on Dad's desk at the police station.

I was always doing that; leaving it at home or elsewhere.

Warren and I waited expectantly until Georgia caught her breath. Meanwhile, all she did was pass her phone to us. It was a local Facebook group post from two hours earlier.

We watched the short video in silence. The cawing of seagulls on the clip made an eerie backdrop. Someone had uploaded it within the last half hour — her young daughter at the end of the pier, done up in a thick jumper with a matching beanie and gloves. Other figures were in the background looking back toward the shore.

The sea was at high tide in the background, a pewter grey in the pale December sun. The time stamp showed that the images were taken on Sunday afternoon, two days before.

Suddenly an old-fashioned sailing ship appeared from nowhere, a ghostly apparition that coalesced into solidity, and moved about thirty yards to the right before vanishing as if it had never been there.

'What the . . . ?' Warren exclaimed. 'It must be a fake. Trick photography.'

Georgia, who had recovered by this time, doubted it, stating that the post was by the administrator and any subterfuge would destroy the prominent public figure's credibility.

'May I?' Warren inquired, asking to hold the smartphone closer to himself. Halfway through the playback, he paused then expanded the image of the wooden vessel.

'It's a corvette.'

I interrupted.

'I thought a Corvette was an American sports car.'

'It is,' Warren agreed, 'but it was a French ship before Napoleon then the Brits started to adopt the name. See the single-gun deck? I reckon late eighteen hundreds, probably sailing north to Sunderland Point or Glasson Dock up towards Lancaster.'

We two females gaped at him. His explanation was directed at my sister, though.

'Georgia. I'm guessing that you have an eye for special antiques from car boot sales or eBay that you can sell on. Me, I study military history. And before you ask, I don't play war games with tiny metal soldiers although I do confess to building model planes and boats in my youth.

'Here, look at the white ensign with the Union Jack in the upper canton. Royal Navy on coastal patrol.'

My sister answered on behalf of us all.

'OK, I'm convinced. Doesn't solve the big question, though, Warren. Why is a century old ship appearing off the coast of Southport?'

He shrugged his impressive shoulders.

'Haven't got the foggiest, ladies. It's a mystery and there's no mistake. The bigger question is, what other strange phenomena will happen next?'

It was then that my two companions noticed my expression and pallid face.

'Cindy? What's up with you, babe? You look like you've seen a ghost.'

'Not a ghost, exactly, Georgia,' I muttered weakly. 'Play the video again but this time zoom in on the two people standing at the far end behind the toddler, facing away from the ship and sea.'

I sat there mutely as they did so. Georgia gasped first.

'It's Amber . . .'

'And you, Cindy,' Warren added. 'But what does this mean?'

I paused, gathering my thoughts as best I could. We hadn't seen the ship but had noticed others reacting to something on the ocean. By the time we turned, the ship had vanished.

I'd assumed that it was a dolphin or whale which had caused the stir. My companions were silent, expecting a response from me.

'It means that all of those visions that I've seen through my life weren't just my imagination, Georgia. They were real and now others can see them, too, even a camera.'

Georgia apologised for poking fun at me all those years before when I'd foolishly raved about my visions with others before I learned to keep my own counsel.

'I'm so sorry, Cindy. I never suspected that you were telling the truth. But what does it mean, you being so close to this hole in time on the pier?'

'By itself, nothing. Yet, I had another vision yesterday morning in Hesketh Park. Just before I met you, Warren.'

'What of?' he inquired.

'You and I ten years ago. Our first . . . and only kiss.'

'Oh,' he said, quietly.

'So,' Georgia continued. 'Two holes in time in your proximity. I still don't understand, Cindy.'

I lifted my gaze from my clasped hands on the white linen tablecloth to fix my gaze on her puzzled expression.

'It means, my darling sister, that those holes in time that I call Elsewhens are becoming stronger and . . .'

'And what, babe?' Her voice betrayed her growing anxiety.

I had to face the truth but this time I needed to share my thoughts with the two people whom I trusted most with my secret and my concerns.

'And these Elsewhens — they're coming for me.'

7

Georgia drove me to Mum's to collect Amber before ferrying us to our home. The Love Affair had one car park space in with the rent. She parked her Mazda there.

As for Warren, he made his excuses and left. No plans for another rendezvous. Not even a civil goodbye. It was as if his mind was elsewhere all of a sudden; concentrating on the kidnap victim, no doubt. Wherever it was, I wasn't invited. He went to pay the bill then left without a word or a wave.

Georgia noted his rudeness, dismissing it with a few words.

'He's a man plus he's Australian. What more can you expect, Cindy?'

I was disappointed. No, more than that — I was downright angry with him. We'd been getting on like a house on fire — at least, that's what I thought.

Once at my apartment, I busied myself

with Amber's meal and bath. Devina was due up at seven for a night of chilli con carne with rice and a bottle of red.

I'd decided to share the video from the pier and confess that I saw through time. It would either be the finish of our friendship when she politely excused herself with some feeble excuse, or the beginning of a closer bond.

I hoped for the latter but, whatever happened, that bottle would be empty by midnight.

Dad had rung Georgia earlier to inform her that he'd found my phone. He intended to return it around seven on his way home. He'd never been to our bijou flat since we moved in. Mum had been twice. Maybe they disapproved.

In any case, Devina was madly frying onions and meat while I opened a tin of kidney beans when he buzzed the intercom from downstairs in the lobby.

I was grateful that she and I shared a similar taste in food. Surprisingly she wasn't a big fan of traditional Indian spicy meals, only the desserts. She blamed it on too many Big Macs as a teenager, messing up her taste buds.

I pressed the button to unlock the security door and waited with my door open until he arrived in the lift. Amber was already in her PJs and sitting in her bedroom, colouring in.

'Dad. Come in. Thanks for bringing my phone over.'

'Sorry, Cindy. I can't stay.'

His face was gaunt. I doubted that he'd eaten properly since the news of the abduction reached his ears. I grabbed his hand and literally dragged him into our two-bed home. He'd been avoiding this for far too long.

In the kitchen, I introduced him to Devina. She turned from the stove.

'So, this is your dad. I was beginning to think he was a figment of your imagination. Pleased to meet you, Chief Inspector Powers.'

Dad was trapped. Finally, he accepted his fate.

'Call me Dave, please.'

Hearing his voice, Amber appeared

from her room and ran to hug my father.

'Grandad!' she said.

'Hello, sweetheart.' He knelt down to her level. 'My. You've grown so much.' I could sense his discomfort although thankfully, Amber didn't.

I was tempted to say that he'd only seen her twice since we moved in and that little girls do grow quickly and he shouldn't blame her for what Jimmy did to me.

I didn't. Instead, I and Mum had concocted a plan to have him engage with his granddaughter more.

'Why not read Amber her bedtime story tonight, Dad? You've got time, haven't you?'

'Please, Grandad,' Amber beseeched him.

I handed him the children's book that Mum had found in the attic. He took it.

'Where did you get this, Cindy? It was your favourite.'

'You used to read it to me all the time.'

Nodding mutely, he ushered Amber into her bedroom, staring at the book.

'And don't forget the funny voices, Dad. She'll love those.'

His parting chuckle told me that he understood. He and I needed this but mostly it was for Amber. She needed the same loving, supportive man in her life that he'd been in mine.

As I heard him reading and Amber engaging with her sound effects as she mimicked his, I dialled Mum on the phone he'd returned.

'Dad will be a bit late for dinner, Mum,' I informed her as I rejoined Devina in preparing our meal for tonight. Dad emerged quite a while later, gently closing Amber's door behind him as he switched off the big light.

'She's smart, Cindy. Reminds me of you. Thanks for your not-so-gentle push, too. I needed that.'

I embraced him. One step at a time. There were far too many lost years to make up between my family and us.

'Take tomorrow off, Dad. At least the morning. No buts. Your SIC can handle things and if she can't, she'll contact you.'

Dad hesitated to agree. His work ethic and desire to find Bart Travis alive drove him but it consumed him far more than it should.

'I'd love to Cindy, but . . .'

'Dad. You can't protect everyone . . . especially if you're too ill from overwork. Mum tells me that you've built up a great team. Now's the time to let them fly.'

He agreed, asking when I'd become so mature. The sad answer was that my choices in life were the reason. Wrong choices teach you much more than the right ones.

Tonight, I'd tell Devina of my visions and show her the phone footage which Georgia sent. Tomorrow I'd share my secret with my parents.

* * *

Arriving early at my parents with Amber the following morning, I was pleased when Dad opened the door. He wore slippers and was freshly shaved and

85

showered.

He'd rung the station and was assured that progress was being made in his absence. There had been no ransom demand as yet, but the kidnappers had advised Bart's family that he was alive and well even though he was being held against his will.

There had been two proof-of-life photos with him holding an up-to-date newspaper. Even so, in these modern days of CGI and ease in faking photographs, the old attitude of acceptance of such images was treated sceptically.

Last night's sharing of my tunnel vision through time was accepted by Devina. She explained that the Eastern attitude to all things supernatural was more fluid than Westerners. I never thought she'd be a problem. My parents, though — they were a different matter.

Explaining that this wasn't going to do a quick drop-off of Amber and that I had things to confess were accepted with concern. Whilst Amber watched telly in the other room, I sat with my parents feeling quite apprehensive.

I started by sharing the Facebook video of Amber and me in the background watching the photographer's daughter. She and I were oblivious to the appearance of the ghostly corvette in the ocean behind us. By the time we realised that spectators were pointing and shouting, the ship had vanished back into its own time.

Dad and Mum watched and showed surprise, Dad even commenting that several other strange apparitions had been reported to the police during the week.

I sat forward to address them, fearful of what they'd say.

Dad spoke first after I related everything about my Elsewhen experiences, including Monday morning in the park. There had been one of those so-called pregnant pauses where the sole sound was the television.

'I'm sorry, love, but you cannot expect rational people like your mother and I to accept ...'

Mum turned to him, grasping his

hands in hers.

'Be quiet, Dave. It's true. Lord help me but it's true ... every single word. I've seen them myself. Or at least I used to, before my mother convinced me that I was imagining things. When our Cindy began to see the same, I did what my mother did. And I was so wrong.'

Dad and I stared at my mother, our mouths agape in shock. All of those conversations, telling me that I must be mistaken and not to tell anyone what I'd seen yet all of that time, Mum knew the truth.

My initial thoughts were those of betrayal by the one person I trusted. Then my rational brain took over.

'Granny Tibbs. She was a right old battle axe, wasn't she, Mum? I was so scared of her. You were, too. I remember her telling me I was mad and forcing you to back her up when I described my visions.'

Mum appeared reticent to agree at first but decided to speak her long-suppressed mind.

'You're right. The years that I hated what she did to me . . . Then, because I was so weak, I allowed her to treat you in the same way, telling me that denying your visions was for your own good.

'I honestly believed that, like me, you suppressed them for so long that they ceased to plague you any longer. From what you just said, they didn't go away.'

Mum was crying now at what she'd done to me. It wasn't her fault. Dad remained quiet before picking up my phone again. Reaching out for their iPad, he typed in the website address and sat to watch the offending video on the larger screen.

'One hundred ninety-one comments.' He scrolled through them.

'A few sceptics but there are over thirty people who saw it too, mostly from further down the pier just over Marine Drive. It's one thing if you ladies see things that happened years ago because you're psychics, but for ordinary folk? Photos and videos, too?'

'Dad. I call them Elsewhens — holes

89

in time. I don't think people can go through them but there's something unique about Southport that permits it.

'Almost as if the pages of the past accidentally touch the present for a few moments, like autumn leaves falling from different trees and being blown against your face by a gusty wind.'

He nodded sagely, accepting what I said as gospel. People seeing ghosts of the past was one thing; tangible proof quite another.

'And do these people from decades ago see us? If so, it'd be mighty scary.'

I considered it. What if a man — a scientist even — from nineteen hundred saw the Red Arrows zooming overhead as they did at the local Air Show in July. Or the Typhoon fighter? These things amazed me and Amber and we knew they were real.

'You're dead right, Dad. The truth is that I honestly have no idea. I've never seen into the future. Have you, Mum?'

'Me? No. Never.' She dried her eyes.

'In any case,' Dad wondered, struggling

to accept this very unexpected revelation, 'do you have any idea of the reason this is happening so much at present?'

I hesitated before deciding that, if I were to decipher this puzzle, I needed help.

'It might sound conceited but I'm convinced I'm like the epicentre of this time quake where the past and present are mingling.

'I was present on Southport pier when the corvette appeared and on Monday, I saw myself and Warren when we first kissed. These Elsewhens are trying to grab my attention.'

Dad was treating this like a crime.

'Are you implying something supernatural is intelligent, guiding these Elsewhen thingies to stalk you?'

I dismissed his speculation with reasoned logic. I'd had more opportunity to make sense of it, after all.

'No, Dad. I'm inclined to believe that Christmas is a special time when miracles happen. Maybe it's all this anticipation, joy and positivity? I'm just guessing. If

I had to speculate, these Elsewhens are searching me out to put something right, a hiccup in reality that happened in my past and is happening now.

'I hate to suggest it but Warren being here points to one thing . . . the abductions.'

Mum stared at us blankly.

'That poor William Lockstone, was it? The young man who died because he didn't have his insulin?' she wondered aloud. 'And now Bart Travis?'

'Yes, Kathy,' Dad agreed.

'It was around ten years ago, wasn't it? Back then when you use to write those diaries so religiously every night, Cindy. Without fail. I found a box of them in the attic when I was searching for books for Amber to read. Funny this is, I had a dream about you writing in those diaries last night.'

No. It couldn't be a coincidence, could it?

Both Mum and me dreaming about the same thing.

'Mum. Last night, I dreamed about

writing them too. Maybe these Else-whens aren't always strong enough to make a hole in time that we see through. Maybe they're merely able to nudge our minds when we're asleep? I don't suppose . . .'

She and Dad perked up from the morose state they were in. Dad was the one who spoke.

'We'll fetch them down today for you to read, love. There must be a clue in there.'

For the sake of Bart Travis, I truly hoped that there was.

8

That it was the festive season wasn't lost on me. The time of miracles was so special for many people. It was a fine, icy drizzle this morning yet, as I walked under the awnings over the Lord Street shops, I noted that people were out enjoying the ambience.

Certainly, the customers weren't sitting outside at the numerous pavement cafés, but they were there, sipping their hot chocolates with gingerbread or cinnamon. Maybe mulled wine, too, although it was a bit early for that for me.

Even if it were more comfortable to be tucked up inside where warm air caressed their skin, many relished the exhilaration of braving the winter, possibly harkening back to those days of Charles Dickens' 'A Christmas Carol' where everybody was swathed in woollen coats and scarves.

True, they might have their hands

in pockets, grasping an electric hand warmer as their teeth chattered, but the thought of this universal special time of the year kept their spirits up.

'Merry Christmas,' a total stranger said as she passed by, a smile on her lips.

'And to you,' I replied.

Yeah. Christmas was a time I was beginning to fall in love with again now that I was back home and free of Jimmy's oppressive influence.

Our shop was enjoying the increased trade from Christmas shoppers. I saw many familiar faces from my youth, people I'd not engaged with for years. It was a little sad to see them being noticeably older, some now struggling with those ailments associated with age.

Chatting and catching up was part of the experience for them as well as for me. I'd forgotten how much I loved people and sharing the adventures of their lives. Smiling and laughing again was great therapy.

My former science teacher arrived around half-eleven with her grown-up daughters. Yvonne and I became friends years ago. It was unusual for a teacher/pupil but she'd sought me out after I graduated.

I considered approaching her now about my spectral Elsewhen visions, yet felt silly. Besides, the social media had already forgotten all about the corvette ship.

The latest trending posts were about the antics of the Savitski-trained cats that could do all sorts of miraculous tricks. Those led to other posts about Southport kitty wannabes trying the emulate their world-famous cousins.

Whoever said yesterday's news was today's chip wrappers probably summed it up back then before health and safety said putting greasy battered fish into newsprint was a definite no-no.

Yvonne was a down-to-earth woman who didn't even read the daily horoscopes that I doted on. The three of them appeared content to browse the displays at their leisure, discussing amongst themselves objects that took their fancy.

She and I had similar tastes in those special knick-knacks that transformed a house into a home. Her daughters also shared those attitudes as they carried their selections to the cash desk.

As the others finished their purchases, Yvonne took me to one side.

'I'm impressed. You and Georgia have a special place here. You've moved on from Jimmy. Time to spread your angel wings, girl.'

I giggled.

'Hardly a girl, Yvonne. Those days are gone . . . wasted.'

'I never liked him, you realise.'

I was surprised and showed it.

'You never said.'

'Not my place, love. You adored him and I didn't have the heart to put our friendship in jeopardy. Your family voiced their opinions about him and I saw the rift that caused.'

That was astute and sadly true. Back then Lucinda Powers was a stubborn person, convinced that they were all mistaken. When I did eventually split up

97

with Jimmy and left, they'd welcomed me back but my relationship with family, even Georgia, had been quite rocky for too long.

At least now we were getting along. I could have blamed Jimmy for driving a wedge between us but I was the one who was at fault, thinking that I had all the answers. Hindsight was a wonderful talent but, just like my gift of seeing through those Elsewhen windows, knowing about mistakes from the past hadn't helped present-day me at all.

'Anyway, Jimmy's out of my life. I just wish I had more sense back then.'

We perused other gifts in cases and on show, wandering through nooks and crannies back to the waiting girls. Yvonne complimented us on how we'd transformed the shop. Today, it was a cosy maze instead of the bright, impersonal box it had been in its previous incarnation as part of a large department store closed due to 'progress' and new online shopping.

Georgia had achieved a knock-down

price for renting it on the basis that any rental money is better than nothing. The council helped, too, eager to increase footfall into the pedestrian precinct. Furthermore, we'd opened about three months before Christmas; a golden time of the year for sales.

At the desk, Yvonne asked, out of the blue, if romance was on my life's horizon.

'Strange that you should ask. The answer is no. Amber is my life now. We'll have to have a proper catch-up soon. She's shot up so much since you last saw her. Why did you ask about whether I had anew guy in my life?'

I guessed the answer to her not-so-subtle hint before she had a chance to say it. She'd heard about Warren returning.

'I always thought that you and he would move past the best friend's stage. From what I hear on the local grapevine, he's quite a hunk these days, Cindy.'

I was amazed at how quickly gossip spread. The word hunk wasn't right, either. It was dated. Warren was much more than a hunk, anyway. He was bright as well. No doubt our perfectly innocent drinks at the Kaleidoscope had been spread by Southport gossip.

'Reports of anything more than a friendly tête-à-tête have been exaggerated, Yvonne. Sorry to disappoint you.'

'Pity. He loved you back then and I was kind of hoping an engagement party might be the perfect excuse to purchase a cute dress I've seen in Pandalfo's.'

'Engagement!' I spluttered. 'As if. Anyway, he's just visiting his grandparents over Christmas.'

I crossed my fingers behind my back about the little white fib regarding the reason for his visit to Britain. The very idea of an engagement shocked me and I wondered what had possibly prompted such an outrageous suggestion from my normally very down-to-earth friend.

I chose to change the slightly upsetting conversation. Warren's reaction (or lack thereof) when he left me the evening before, had upset me. Although there was no reason that it should have, it did . . . and that was that.

'Have you heard about Bart Travis being abducted? He was in my class.'

Yvonne rubbed her chin.

'I heard about it, but can't recall him or his face. Consider how many students I've taught since your days.'

She had a point. I always was amazed how she managed to remember the names in each year she taught.

'One thing I heard on the radio before we came out, though — the amount the criminals are asking for the ransom. A cool two million.'

I gasped.

'Two million pounds?'

'What's stranger is that they're not keeping it a secret.'

She was right. Usually, the perpetrators (or perps as Dad called them) avoided publicity about their intentions. This crew were revelling in it, involving papers, telly and the radio. They'd done it already ten years before and managed to escape with the money. Sadly, William had paid the price due to his illness. I prayed that Bart wouldn't end up in the same situation.

Yvonne glanced at her watch and realised that her parking time was almost up. We said a hasty farewell to her and the girls, leaving me contemplating her words about Warren and me. Would it hurt to give him a bell?

Before I was able to give it any more thought, another blast from the past entered the shop and headed straight for me. Keith Giffen, my school mate from The Kaleidoscope, was on a mission. His cheery face and rosy cheeks reminded me of his long-time nickname of Saint Nick as Keith had always been a Santa in training.

'Cindy!' he exclaimed, his eyes wide and that exuberance of his almost scary in its intensity. 'So lovely to see you again. Positively lovely.'

He took me in his arms giving loud air kisses to both sides of my face. I accepted it grudgingly. Keith was simply being Keith.

'I'm sorry that I missed you and your

man friend yesterday, duckie. Heaven knows I spend almost every day in my lovely shop but even I need a break now and then to see Mater and Pater and shoot the breeze with them. How's the new venture?'

He took a moment to survey the shop and customers as I perused my long-time flamboyant friend. Pink faux fur edging on his long white coat — yep, Keith was never going to change.

'Oh. Busy, busy, busy, I see. How lovely for you. I wish that my little venture into the commercial hustle and bustle of commerce was as busy but hey-ho. I love what I do and that is so crucial to karma and a beautiful life, isn't it?'

Keith was upset, despite his bravado. I'd known him long enough to realise that. He was never this OTT except when he was in trouble. Leaning towards me, he whispered into my ear, the barest whiff of alcohol detectable on his breath. Even for Keith, this was too early.

'May I have a word in your shell-like, duckie? In private, seal vouz play?'

Keith's poor attempt at speaking French confirmed my suspicions. Family troubles.

Keith lived for his shop and had never bothered with any romantic entanglements so the one thing left in his life was family.

'Sure, Keith. Out back?'

'Lovely,' he said as I led the way, signalling to Georgia that I needed five and then, on second thoughts, ten minutes.

Once away from the gaze of others, he began to cry, recovering quickly to reassume his flamboyant persona. He reached into his coat to produce a matching pink hankie which he dabbed to his eyes. Honestly. Keith and his faux furs.

'Pater is very upset at the low turnover from my magnificent butterfly restaurant. He's talking about closing it down.' A final sob escaped his lips before he turned to me for help.

What could I suggest? His father had indulged his sole child about the time he left school by buying and redecorating the once-popular restaurant.

'Keith. Perhaps a change of décor? Not everyone appreciates butterflies as much as you. More muted colours — low romantic lighting? Let's face it. Fluttering wings as you're tucking into a steak or chicken risotto is . . . well, a tad disconcerting.'

'But I love my butterflies, Cindy.'

'And that's fine for you. Can't you be content with that heated greenhouse of them in your backyard? You could still keep the name, though. The Kaleidoscope doesn't just mean a gathering of butterflies, does it?'

'I suppose that you might have a point.' He was morose and clearly disappointed with my advice. Keith — well, let's simply say that he had issues with reality at times.

'What's prompted your dad being concerned with turnover all of a sudden, anyway? He's never bothered before.'

Keith became a little defensive at that point.

'Listen. Forget I said that. Pater doesn't

want me to discuss finances with any-one, especially you, Cindy. You're the last friend I really have from the old days. Having you back in Southport and in my life again has meant so much. Jimmy never phones these days so it's just you, sweetie.'

I tried to comfort him as much as I could. Moreover, there was that slip of the tongue about sharing his father's seeming lack of financial liquidity at the moment.

'Especially you, Cindy'? What did that mean? OK, Keith's 'Pater' and I had always had issues, possibly due to my dad's occupation, but that had always been the case with kids at school. Being a copper's daughter wasn't conducive to being the centre of attention. Warren had always been the exception and now, with him back on the scene, I needed to repair those issues between us.

Keith left soon afterwards but not before doing another strange thing. We had a charity box on the counter. When Keith noticed it, he took out his wallet and a fifty-pound note then pushed it in.

'That's a lot of money, Keith,' I suggested, concerned that he wasn't thinking straight.

'It's for a good cause, right? That's important to me, these days. Don't be a stranger, Cindy. Bring your new friend in for a meal sometime.

'Oh yes, almost forgot. Is it OK to put a flyer in your window for The Kaleidoscope? Any little bit helps, doesn't it?' He took one from the leather folder he'd been carrying. He was doing the rounds.

'Sure.' I put it on the counter. 'I'll stick it in a prominent place. Perhaps here by the till. People will be waiting to be served and have more chance to read it properly.'

He nodded and left. Georgia, who'd been watching, came over.

'Fifty squid, Cindy? What was that about?'

I gazed at the plastic container, wondering the same thing.

'Just feeling generous . . . Guilty

conscience . . . Who knows?'

For one scant moment, I had a horrible thought, before dismissing it out of hand. Life was complicated enough at the present without adding to my anxieties.

Keith was right about one thing, though. Warren and I needed to meet again in a leisurely atmosphere, sit down and have one of those deep, soul-bearing discussions.

When the day ended, I went back to our kitchen area to ring Warren. Unfortunately, the call was short and not so sweet. I didn't have his mobile so, rather than bother Dad, I called his grandparents. My expectation that they would share it with me was a big mistake.

The words echoed in my mind long after his grandfather had hung up. The vileness in his voice shocked me to my soul.

'Cindy Powers? You have some nerve, lady. After what you did to Warren, you can go jump. None of us wants anything to do with you ever again.'

9

Devina was busy that night, working on a thesis or dissertation or something important that was time sensitive. I wasn't really in a hospitable mood so it worked out well . . . for her anyway.

Warren's family were such lovely people. It was bad enough that I'd hurt Warren by not believing him back then, but I never considered them. Once Warren returned to the colonies, I dismissed them, as had my family. It was wrong, but we perceived Warren's unfounded betrayal as a reflection upon them, too.

My plan was a quiet night in with Amber. Once she was asleep, I'd be able to read those diaries Mum discovered in the expectation of making sense of the kidnappings and those Elsewhen appearances.

The two were connected. I felt it so strongly. All I needed was a chance to sort through all the other dramas in my life and focus.

A page into the first of my memoirs and I gave up. My mind was awash with questions and anguish over the attitude of Warren's family. Also, why had he walked away the previous evening after viewing the video with me and the corvette ship?

Seeking something to numb my brain, I chose a combination that did the job for me — wine and a Midsomer. I prided myself on guessing the murderers before super-sleuth Inspector Barnaby. Strangely, that's what the show was called in France where half the population probably believed that every town in Britain was exactly like the Midsomer ones (without multiple murders each week, presumably). My brain must have still been distracted as I picked the wrong murderer completely. What a disappointment.

★ ★ ★

I'd hardly had a chance to get warm after arriving next day when Georgia summoned me to the phone. It was Devina. She sounded quite distressed, apologising that she'd tried in vain to ring my mobile without success. I checked it. It was on mute, for some reason. More concerning was the subdued panic in her voice.

My mind immediately jumped to all sorts of conclusions: a fire? A break-in? She quickly reassured me. There had been an incident but it was under control. She did need to speak with me in person, though.

'I've just arrived in town, Devina. Do you want me to go home again?'

'No, Cindy. Sorry. I'm in the Atkinson library. Five minutes?'

'OK. But it had better be good.' I hated to take advantage of my fellow workers' accommodating nature but Georgia had promised they'd have my back, accepting that I was the centre of some major dramas at present.

The walk to the library took less than

five and Devina was waiting for me in the foyer outside, a bag full of papers and books in hand. She needed to complete her uni work today using research sources here.

Devina could spare me a short time. ordered drinks from the café just outside the library as she delved into her bag and lay a dozen or so identical posters on the tabletop. I gasped.

No wonder she was upset. So was I.

Devina wanted confirmation in words, though.

'Is this it? That horrible flyer you told me about? The one from school?'

'Yes. It is.'

'They were plastered all over the foyer and stuffed in some mailboxes. I managed to fish them out.'

I expressed my heartfelt gratitude to Devina. I hated to believe that my neighbours might think badly of me even though I was hardly to blame. Devina continued.

'I don't think any residents noticed them as I ripped them down right away. I checked when I saw a suspicious woman hanging around the front of our block.'

'Devina. Can you describe the lady you saw?'

'Furtive, ponytail, mid-twenties with a bright green beanie, 'I'm so awesome' written on the back of her leather jacket. Recognise her?'

Taking a moment to reflect, I gazed out the window overlooking Lord Street. Outside, the drizzling rain had seemingly settled in.

Hearing her detailed information, I realised exactly who was to blame. I clenched my fists, angrily facing Devina as our drinks and snacks were brought on a tray.

'Oh yeah. A scumbag who fortunately hasn't learnt the art of not being conspicuous. Let me tell you all about her.'

Shania blinking Featherly, ex-bestie and long-time lover of my ex-husband was about to discover that I wasn't the meek, timid woman I'd once been.

'Sexy' Shania had always been good-looking, right from her days in tutu dresses at the same ballet classes I went to. She was quite aware of her stunning looks as all her family doted on her, reinforcing that belief that she was pretty as a princess. That's why it surprised me that she went out of her way to befriend me. I was grateful for the attention.

Unlike Shania with her natural effervescence, I was shy and conscious that my copper-toned locks signalled me out for other reasons. Yeah — it's a fine distinction between strawberry-blonde and carrot-top. I fought a losing battle for far too long.

OK, it was the freckles and pale skin more than the hair. And being the skinny, tallest girl in my class never helped much, either. I simply wanted to be normal and blend in with the crowd.

Devina had her different battles to fight but, unlike many when I broke up with Jimmy, she accepted me as a friend.

Her advice taught me the truth; Shania the liar never had my best interests at heart. I sort of suspected that once she gleefully declared that she and Jimmy had been seeing one another since well before our marriage.

Devina showed me that Shania's sinister behaviour went far further back than when we left school. Subtle comments like, 'That colour doesn't do you justice, Cindy' to more direct statements like 'Honestly, I wouldn't be seen dead in that. Why not buy this one that I've chosen?'

And, like a fool I did. My choice of a dress was discarded and her choice purchased with my money. She convinced me to buy those miniskirts when I always felt they made me look cheap. Worse still, I wore them at her behest, always uncomfortable and feeling others were laughing at me silently or making snide comments.

Then Devina pointed out in my old photos that Shania always wore more demure clothing and less flamboyant makeup.

Devina asked me a question I'd also been wondering about for months. If Jimmy fancied Shania so much then why marry me? Sadly, the answer wasn't that difficult to suss out.

Money. Gran's money. Not that I'd be a zillionaire or anything but that trust fund she'd set up in my name was enough to tempt the gold-digging, slimy rodent . . . and his floozy.

In true Cindy Powers fashion, my schoolgirl self inadvertently let slip to Shania that I was coming into an inheritance. Even told her the amount. I mean how mind-numbingly dumb was that? Soon after, Jimmy began taking a greater interest in me, said all the right things, romancing my socks off Miss Naivety 2015 and before I knew it, Jimmy was my loving husband for better, for worse, for richer — definitely for richer.

When he learnt that I could only access the fund at the age of twenty-eight, he was not best pleased. Had Gran foreseen that we'd be divorced when I was twenty-six? In retrospect, I believe that she did, protecting me and her inheritance from beyond the grave.

Oh, sure, he fought his hardest to

keep us together but his philandering ways were his undoing. Even I was capable of hiring a private detective. They'd covered their tracks for years in a cleverly devised subterfuge to keep me in the dark.

But when it led to a confrontation with videos, photos and dates of illicit liaisons, the years of lies unravelled like a ball of wool.

Devina gently shook my shoulder.

'Day-dreaming again, Cindy? Let me guess . . . a new way of torturing Shania?'

'How can you tell?'

'Doesn't matter. But you've been hurt a lot by their behaviour. If you show some anger over what they did, even months after the divorce, it's OK by me. Just remember that I'm here for you.'

We briefly discussed the implications of Shania coming back into my life to deliver that document from way back then. I had prayed that, after the divorce, they'd leave me alone. I mean, they lived nowhere near Southport, last thing I heard.

Even before we wed, Jimmy couldn't wait to get out of our town and away from his family and mine. In hindsight, I should have suspected that his parents saw the truly nasty side of him long before I did.

Although I loved it here, he insisted that we move and just like with Shania, I let him dictate my life choices.

'What if they heard that you and the Aussie met up again? From what you've told me, your ex-bestie has mates in town. All it needs was one blabbermouth to share your mum's post about you and Warren.

'It figures that they'd want to make any relationship involving you fail. What better way than to remind you of his betrayal, especially if you didn't realise who sent it?'

I nodded.

'Devina. You're so clever.'

'Nah. I just think the same devious way as them. Face it, love. You're too much of an innocent. Me, I grew up in a dog-eat-dog neighbourhood with a mum who couldn't care less. I survived and once I finish my degree, I'm going places well away from that past that dragged me down. But right now, I need to nip out to the Ladies.'

When she returned, I noted the time on the café clock.

'Sorry, Devina. I'm stopping you from that research. Selfish of me.'

'Not at all. I needed the mind-fog break. Actually, after you rang, I did some research into those strange time holes. And it paid off. Look at this.'

She passed me a photocopy of a ship's log; the *HMS Amethyst*. It was a twenty-six-gun Spartan class ship from the mid eighteen hundreds, according to the footnotes, captained by Ephraim Kitterstone Esquire.

I read it aloud.

'On this day, June the seventh, 1851, First Mate Horatio Bakerleigh and I did espy asight most distressing, for where there be nothing but for the wide beach near Penfold Channel and Angry Brow, a pier, exceeding long, did exist reaching out from Southport township that be shrouded in fog most obscure.

'With spyglass in hand, I did examine strangely garbed persons promenading there on. Mister Bakerleigh confirmed my observations, indicating in addition, the presence of a minuscule train moving along the pier. Of smoke from the chimney, there was no sign which be most discombobulating.

'As quickly as it did appear, the image did revert to bright sunshine as is the want of clement June weather. Of the pier, there did remain no sign. Mister Bakerleigh and I are neither of us dauncy nor have we partaken of our ration of rum afore our watch and I record this sighting most worryful in the expectation that there be an explanation forthcoming.'

'Well?'

'Well, for starters, I'll never say you talk funny again, Devina. Clearly, they saw us just like we saw them.'

'Time paradox. That's why time travel only works for funny doctors in police boxes or strange American shows on telly or at the cinemas. It's better to believe that all the people who have seen the ship are all sharing mass hallucinations.'

'With video proof,' I added sarcastically.

'CGI, Cindy? It makes more sense than time travel. Believe me.'

'Yeah. You're right. But don't forget that I've seen these Elsewhen visions many times, too.'

She laughed gently.

'Let's see what your Elsewhen visions have to say about the future of your life.'

10

The remainder of the day was a mixture of keeping myself busy in The Love Affair and inwardly seething at Shania if I had a moment of peace in between assisting customers and restocking.

Not content with humiliating me through my school years and then stealing my husband's affections, she was back with her sneaky machinations.

Naturally, I confided the poster situation to Georgia, expecting a profound suggestion for my next step regarding revenge. But my younger sister simply told me to get over it.

'Pardon?' I exclaimed.

'In the grand scheme things, with poor Bart being held for ransom, a few pictures isn't much to worry about.'

* * *

The chilly evening air as I walked from the bus stop on Manchester Road froze me back to normality. My revenge was on hold . . . at least for the evening. Seeing Dad's car in my parents' drive, I quickened my pace to the front door of the big Victorian semi so common in the seaside resort.

Overhead the moon shone its eerie light through a gathering mist. The flashing-coloured lights on the large Leyland pine outside cheered me immediately; the annoying motion-activated singing child-sized Santa not so much.

That was Mum's doing. She was a real Christmas person whereas Dad was more of a Scrooge type of guy when it came to the OTT decorations sold in local shops since September.

'Hi, everyone. I'm home,' I shouted gleefully as I doffed my overcoat, boots and gloves. Only it wasn't my home. It hadn't been for years.

Mum entered, dressed in the same rose floral pinny she'd worn since I could remember. Amber ran to hug me, dashing quickly past her. Mum's hug was less crushing yet welcome nonetheless.

'Mummy. Mummy. Come see the present Grandpa found upstairs.' She grabbed my hand and tugged me until I complied with a laugh.

It was spread out on the lounge room floor, Dad kneeling as he placed a tiny figure of a horse on to the patterned carpet.

'The old train set? Honestly, Dad.'

To my surprise, Amber knelt and began to play, happily replacing the choo-choo engine when it chose to leave the track. He and my darling girl were engaging. She showed me the bridge over the plastic road that they'd pieced together. What a joy to witness.

'You always did want someone to play trains with, Dad. I'm pleased for you.'

He turned his gaze upward to me and then to Amber who was engrossed joining more track to the as-yet unused siding. I left them to address Mum in the hall.

'Boys and their toys,' she said with a

glance over her shoulder. 'And girls, too, it seems. He needs her.'

'I'm glad they're friends at last. Also, his face. He's ten years younger than the man I saw at the station. So, who convinced him to take a break from this kidnapping case? You, Mum?'

She scoffed.

'Me? Hardly. He's never taken my advice about his overdoing it. Whoever it was, I owe them. Truth is, I suspect you confessing to these Elsewhen visions of yours helped, Cindy.

'His team will continue the search without him. They're a great bunch, well taught. This case, though . . . It's a very strange one.'

We entered the kitchen. Mum had a roast on the bench and vegetables on the stove and in the oven. She lit the burner under the gravy, asking me to stir whilst she carved the joint of beef.

'Yorkshires?' I asked, savouring the aroma of the honey-glazed carrots as she opened the oven to check on them.

'There's more than enough for you

two if you're in no rush to go home, love.'

In the past, I made my excuses, not wanting to intrude too much on our still tenuous relationship. Jimmy had estranged me from them and until we moved back to Southport, they'd seen Amber a handful of times in the first four years of her life. Being asked to share a meal tonight felt right, though.

'That would be super, if it's not too much bother, Mum.'

'No bother at all, Lucinda. Watch that gravy now whilst I tell Dave and Amber. Does she like Yorkshire puddings?'

I pondered that momentarily.

'You know, I don't believe she's ever had them. You know I'm no cook. Maybe that's why Jimmy . . .'

'No. Jimmy had his reasons for hurting you, love, as well you know. Your amazing talent to carbonise every meal are not why he destroyed your life. You have so many other strengths and abilities.

'Now. A bottle of wine? Dad won't partake whilst he's on call and I hate to drink alone.'

As we finished our meal (with seconds in one or two cases), I sat back, satisfied that our derailed relationship was firmly back on track.

Mum suggested a sleepover for Amber in my old bedroom. I accepted but declined the offer to accommodate me as well overnight. I needed me time to read the diaries.

As Mum happily prepared my lovely girl for bed, I had a chance to chat with Dad. I pondered how he managed to keep the unsavoury world of police work from interfering with his home life, dragging him down into the mire which he dealt with every day.

'It's easy to say, Cindy, but hard to maintain. I focus on family when I'm at home. Are you dwelling on your married life even now? I realise that it can't have been easy.'

'No. I moved on, Dad, but today I was almost dragged back into it. The anger — it's hard to cope with.'

'Then turn those bad emotions

around, Cindy.'

He indicated the scattered toys on the floor and the train set. He'd decided to set it up permanently in the attached garage for him and Amber.

'Focus on the good things in your life: the shop, your friend, Devina, Amber, being back in Southport and ...' He paused.

'And what, Dad?' 'Dare I say Warren?' I sat back.

'We're friends. That's all. I thought for a moment that there was something more when I saw him at The Kaleidoscope but I was wrong. The minute he learned about me and my Elsewhen visions he disappeared.'

Dad grinned.

'That was unlike him, Cindy. He loves you. Always has. Probably part of the reason he's back here, to be honest. Nevertheless, he has a job to do, just like me, and you're not a priority.'

Aware of my role as a distraction with the previous kidnapping, I understood that. Shania was doing what she did best — getting under my skin. Yet a part of me wondered if this leaflet resurfacing had a more sinister implication.

I asked my father how he concluded that Warren wasn't to blame for printing the leaflets.

'Alibi. A dozen other students were witnesses to him playing chess in a comp when whoever was busy using his passcode on the school computer and printer.

'By the time I and the staff discovered that, he'd left the country. We never traced the real villain but we did collect all two hundred printed copies.'

I delved into my bag and laid the new copies out on the coffee table.

'Then more have been printed. These were put out in my apartment block this morning. Luckily, Devina collected them before any damage was done. She saw the perp.'

Dad's expression became grim and I instantly regretted involving my parents again.

'Who was he, Cindy? I can deal with him. If he printed these, he must have done the same back in school.'

'He's a she, Dad. Shania Featherly. You remember her, especially when she was at her flirty best. Georgia suggested I ignore her latest provocation; see if she escalates her actions when I don't react.

'I figure that makes sense. If she's involved, chances are Jimmy is, too. But I'm not the same person I was then. I turned to him for support and comfort ten years ago, probably part of his long-term plan to romance me and get Gran's trust fund. I'm hardly likely to rush back into his arms again.'

Dad was busy thinking.

'Jimmy's long-term plan. That's what you said, isn't it? Just like these kidnappers today. They're in no rush to collect their ransom. Not yet, anyway.'

That puzzled me as well. Not that I was privy to the ways of criminals apart from being an avid watcher of 'Midsomer', but most kidnappings were rapid; snatch the victim, ring the family, demand the ransom and collect it, allowing the victim to be returned unharmed. No police, no publicity.

Yet whoever was responsible for Bart's abduction was taking their sweet time, flaunting their crime to the police and media. Was it arrogance or something else?

Dad suggested what I'd already considered and dismissed.

'Is Jimmy responsible for the abduction, Cindy?'

I shuddered. To hear the allegation spoken aloud was upsetting. We were married for goodness' sake. I shared his bed. We had Amber. Was he capable of this horrendous crime?

'I'd wondered, Dad, especially with these leaflets reappearing as a distraction for me and indirectly for you. But no. Jimmy's many things but he hasn't got the brains. Neither has Shania.

'They're manipulative and kept me in the dark about their affair for far too long but this? He was sixteen when William Lockstone was taken and when he died and you or Warren said the crimes

131

are too similar to be copycats. If it's the same crew? No. Not Jimmy.'

Dad put his hand on mine.

'Sorry. I had to ask, sweetheart.'

Following that, I mentioned the cool reception I'd had upon ringing Warren's grandparents. Dad assured me that he'd have a word and smooth things over if Warren hadn't already done that.

We then moved on to brighter issues not long before Mum joined us.

Mum invited us for Christmas lunch. Until tonight, a family get-together hadn't been mentioned and I'd assumed that we'd see them but not eat together. Georgia and Mike were to be invited also; a proper family Christmas. The first since I'd married.

The rest of the evening went quickly, relaxing with wonderful memories and anecdotes from the past, laughs at Dad's old, lame jokes and some new ones too. Despite not drinking, he enjoyed the evening as Mum and I shared a bottle. At eleven-thirty, I made my excuses. Time to leave.

Dad kindly offered to drive me home, suggesting that a sharp frost might make the short walk too treacherous under-foot. I accepted.

He went out to start the car up and clear the screen. Alone with Mum, I inquired about Dad's health.

'Better. Tonight's been a real tonic for him. He forgets that he's not as young as he was and that his passion for helping victims must be tempered with taking care of himself, too. Quite frankly, Cindy, I'm surprised by this change of attitude.

'You sharing those Elsewhen sight-ings of yours led to a real heart-to-heart with him last night. Maybe the shock of yours and my hidden gifts has given him a chance to re-evaluate what life is all about.' She hugged me.

'Don't you worry about Amber, either. She'll be fine tonight with us. Give us a chance to show her how much we both adore her. You're not alone any longer, love.'

The drive back to Leyland Road was a few streets, skirting around the large park and lake in between our homes. It was maybe a ten minute walk along safe streets. Even so, I was grateful for Dad's offer.

Hardly any traffic was around; a few cars and a double-decker bus, possibly the final run for the night. Here and there, houses were bedecked with Christmas lights, glowing reindeer, friendly polar bears and Father Christmases in sleighs.

I saw one dancing lit-up penguin, feeling quite out of place in this pretend North Pole wonderland. Seemingly, the householder hadn't realised that penguins were from the South Pole, but it was hardly their fault. The blame lay with the shops, eager to capitalise on anything from freezing-cold climes. The joy and atmosphere made me happy.

Half dozing, I didn't notice what was ahead immediately but once I did, I screamed for him to stop. He was a trained pursuit driver in an unmarked police car. The brakes squealed, as we lurched forward against the seat belts.

'Wha . . . ?' he turned angrily to me. I

raised one hand and pointed mutely. He gasped as he stared ahead.

'What the hell? Where's the road gone?'

Assuming that it was a rhetorical question, as I had no clue, I tried to process the situation. The car headlights revealed that we'd stopped about ten feet from the hazy edge where the road ceased and a few feet below, a narrow dirt track wended its way through a forest of sparse trees.

Of the rows of houses that should have lined the road, there was no sign.

'Elsewhen,' I said in hushed tones as I opened the door. It was almost dusking in this other time period.

Dad stood out, too, whistling at the sight of the huge height gap between the now road and the then one. A hundred years earlier, probably more.

My knowledge of local history wasn't great but people lived in Churchtown before one of the residents, William Sutton, chose to construct a bathing house near the far end of what soon became Lord Street.

From the unnerving shadows, we heard the sound of horses approaching, still hidden behind the trees on a bend.

Sound as well as a vision. This was a powerful time tunnel, for sure.

'Is this one of those 'time-window' thingies, Cindy?' He advanced to the edge of the road, shimmering in a field of I didn't know what.

Immediately, I cautioned him to stay back. What if he fell into it? Would he be trapped in the past? And if he were would that mean he didn't exist now? Would I ever be born?

The implications rushed through my head as I stared into the near dusk at the approaching horses and riders. Our side of the barrier was almost midnight, a fine drizzle on a cold December night. On the other side, it was late spring, judging from the foliage freshly bursting forth upon the trees. There was a wild rhododendron in bloom, a coral pink among the verdant greens. The air was warm as it touched our faces, again a change from the frigidity of all my other visions.

A butterfly fluttered across the barrier too before falling to the tarmac at our feet. I stared at it, suddenly dead against the frosty surface. Memo to self. Changing times via the Elsewhen was deadly to insects; probably to people, too.

Was it a sign? Dad had his back turned to me but was edging back. The riders, five of them on horseback, had arrived and were staring back at us. We were silhouettes to them, framed by the streetlights with houses where there shouldn't be any. Yet it was the car, headlamps blazing, that terrified them the most.

They weren't intimidated by the car. Quite the opposite. That suggested that the group of men were from the military even though they were not in uniform. I heard the jumble of shouted voices, much of it unintelligible yet one word was clear . . . 'Demon'.

'Dad. We better clear out of here. Now,' I advised my father who was still spellbound by the inexplicable phenomenon.

I had a bad feeling about this. The burly men were quite visible in the glare of the headlights. They began throwing pebbles and hefty rocks towards us and the car. I heard a headlight shatter and a resounding cheer as they blinded the huge monster menacing them.

Another shattered the windscreen with a tinkly crash. Rocks bounced off the bodywork with a loud metallic clang, and then I heard a cry of pain as my dad collapsed on to the roadway.

11

Dad gathered his wits and struggled to his feet, limping badly as he joined me well away from the vehicle, the object of their rage. I feared that they might breach the invisible barrier as had the butterfly and barrage of make-shift weapons, but they didn't. Chances were, they might have died at the attempt.

The Elsewhen disappeared, leaving the road intact before us and a very damaged car. Of the stone-throwing locals, there wasn't any sign.

Although Dad was groaning in pain from the rock that had struck him on the back of the thigh, he was able to hobble around.

'How are you going to explain all of this?' I asked as he produced his phone to call the station.

'Local vandals. I won't mention that they all died decades ago. And before you ask, Cindy, no hospital. It'll hurt but no broken bones. It's almost worth the pain to have witnessed that, whatever it was. Any ideas as to the reason for that little spooky happening?'

I'd been considering that very thing and opened up the plastic box that I used for Amber's fruit snacks. Dad stared at the new contents.

'That butterfly?'

'If these time-windows are happening so often to me and there's a reason behind it, a message for me, then that butterfly appearing seemingly has significance. The men on horses were just bad luck.'

'I agree, Cindy Bear. Especially for my rear end and the car. Wait. Here comes our lift home. I'll have one of the officers drive my car back to the station whilst the other drops us both off.

'Good thing that none of the neighbours noticed anything untoward otherwise we'd be filling in reports until doomsday.'

The police cruiser rolled to a stop behind Dad's police-issue Volvo and we were soon at our respective homes. Dad was headed to a warm, soothing bath and bed whereas I had a date with my school day diaries.

Oh yes, and trying to make sense of the dead blue butterfly.

Even though I read my teenage musings twice, I failed to discern anything that might assist the present situation. They were a tedious litany of ramblings about my school friends and music, often so banal that I wondered if they were written by me at all. I had thought that I was so grown-up.

Nonetheless, in retrospect, I accepted my childishness and realised how easily Shania then Jimmy manipulated me. I didn't mention Warren much in my written musings, apart from my disgust with him at the end of our relationship when I believed he'd betrayed me.

I felt guilty over that, but more so over the indifference to Warren throughout the pages of my then life. We were close, but the words I wrote didn't reflect that. Was I ashamed of what we had?

Possibly.

My sleep was again fitful; my guilty conscience perhaps. Rising in the morning, I realised how much I missed Amber being there. I rang Mum early, who put her on. She was her usual chirpy early morning self, a trait inherited from Jimmy rather than me. Dad was there, too.

He'd shared our homeward adventures and the attack on his car with Mum, making light of the pain. He promised to consult the on-call police doctor although he was far from keen for a woman to examine the growing bruise due to its 'delicate location'.

* * *

Friday morning went well at the shop. The takings overall were much better than we hoped in our business plan, although I was apprehensive about the post-Christmas lull.

Still, we had Saint Valentine's Day and were already planning local

142

advertisements and promotions — Georgia proposed a photo opportunity outside the shop of couples engaged on February fourteenth with a collective celebration with champers and cake.

The idea had merit but Southport weather in late winter was notoriously fickle. Perhaps hiring a hall might be more pleasant, with banners strung around promoting our Love Affair?

I wasn't prepared for Warren arriving. He inquired if I were free for lunch. My Aussie friend was cheery and acted as if nothing bad had happened between us. Suspecting that it was to spare a confrontation in public, I smiled sweetly and agreed.

He suggested The Kaleidoscope; probably because I was comfortable being there. Or maybe it was Keith's promotional flyer on the counter. As it happened, it was a bad decision in one way but useful in the long run. The Fates were playing games with us yet again.

Keith wasn't anywhere in sight as we entered the establishment. Despite having rugged himself up against the wintry weather, Warren was feeling the cold still and was eager to sit by a radiator where he warmed his gloved hands.

I took the opportunity to appraise him as his shivering lessened. When he noticed my amused expression at his reactions, he settled back, avoiding eye contact for the present. He reminded me of a schoolboy caught doing the wrong thing.

'Reckon you're well and truly cheesed at me for the other day. Apologies but you telling us that you were a psycho shocked me a bit, Cindy.'

I kicked his shin under the table.

'Psychic, if you don't mind. Although, on second thoughts, maybe psycho applies as well. Did my father fill you in on the latest news?'

His demeanour became grimmer.

'Shania Featherly? Doesn't surprise me. I was never her greatest fan. Oh, yeah, and before I explain why your revelation upset me, might I assure you that my grandparents look forward to having you and Amber visit for a meal soon? They apologise for their rudeness.'

'I'm glad. I need to apologise to them, too. It's apparent that Shania was the real culprit behind those malicious leaflets. Her days are definitely numbered. So, spill the beans about you suddenly scarpering off.'

We paused to order our meals and drinks then resumed our muted conversation. To be fair, the place was hardly buzzing for the lunch rush. That butterfly wallpaper with the occasional flapping wing was rather off-putting. The presence of that one from last night in my bag didn't dispel that creepiness.

'Here, Cind. Have a squizz at these. I Photographed you the day of our Chrissie kiss.'

Warren removed foolscap-sized photos from his leather briefcase, laying them on the linen cloth in front of me. They were old and handled a lot, judging from their state.

I examined each in turn, intrigued by the sequence that focused on the background rather than my face. What had been slightly out of focus to begin with had been enhanced, probably professionally, knowing Warren's true role in Australia.

I squinted. Could it be?

'That's us. Me and Amber. That's us from Monday in the park watching our teenage selves kissing.'

I stared at the image of us, surrounded by a halo. It was an Elsewhen. As Devina had already surmised from the pier, as well as those horsemen last night, Monday's peek into the past was a two-way thing. Warren had inadvertently captured an image of the future.

I peered over the photographs to Warren, his hands held palm open by the radiator.

'How long have you known?'

'That a woman and girl appeared then disappeared in the background from the sequence I snapped with my camera? Almost straight away.

'If I'd used old-fashioned film, it could be a double exposure. Not so with digital photos. It's been a puzzle to me for all these years. That was until you explained your unique ability to see through these gaps in time. When you mentioned you witnessed our kiss from years earlier, I remembered the photos and went home to check them.

'Just imagine it, Cindy. If Older You had warned Younger You about Shania? About Jimmy? Even about me and you breaking up as we did?' He left the questions unanswered.

'Warren. We weren't ever an item to break up.'

His response shocked me.

'I thought we were. Or at least hoped that you'd realise how I felt.'

Uncomfortable for a moment, I avoided eye contact, peering over to the waitress carrying our meals across between the empty tables. It was a chance to change the tone of this discussion.

The reality was that Warren shared aspects of my ability to peer across time just as the people upon the pier had when they viewed the corvette sailing.

The same applied to my dad last night. Powerful forces were disturbing the very fabric of time around Southport and I was convinced more than ever that it revolved around me and the kidnappings.

I felt humbled but determined to do my best to help save Bart. As our food was presented to us along with the drinks we ordered, one of those wall-mounted mechanical butterflies dotted around the walls moved its artificial wings.

It reminded me of last night's acquisition. I delved into my bag and opened the plastic box to display the contents to Warren.

'Crikey, Cindy. You really have a knack for stimulating a bloke's appetite, don't you.'

I ignored his jibe.

'It flew through an Elsewhen window about twelve hours ago. It's a butterfly, Warren.'

'Reckon the little blighter must feel right at home in this joint. That's probably his brother over there, another

Adonis Blue.' Warren indicated a cardboard replica perched on a painted branch of the mural.

'It's usually found down south, around Kent. Likes chalky soils. Surprised it lived here.' He spoke in between tucking into his cheese and tuna melt as I sat there amazed.

'What are you staring at, Possum?' I'd forgotten his nickname for me — a compliment, he said, because we both had gorgeous faces and cute noses.

'You. I understand that you were a nerd but being an expert on Lepidoptera is pushing it. I thought the guy who owns this restaurant was the only one.' I started to eat my meal, grinning as Warren struggled to bite through a stubborn strand of stretchy cheese.

He laughed.

'Me and insects. You're kidding, right? That one beastie is the only one that I . . .'

He stopped, placing his cutlery on the plate as his brow furrowed.

'When you suggested that your

butterfly appearing from nowhere meant something to the kidnappings, Cindy, you were spot on.' He leant forward to speak in hushed tones.

'You remember that my brief is to re-examine the bloke who died from no insulin? Right?'

'Yes. William Lockstone,' I managed between mouthfuls.

His voice dropped lower.

'I've gone through the file again and again.

One fact that was never released was what was found in his clothing, a sign as to where he was imprisoned. A butterfly. That blinking butterfly.'

'Rubbish. He died late November. There aren't butterflies around then. Too cold.'

'Exactly. An Adonis Blue in a place it shouldn't be and at a time it shouldn't be. But the truth is in front of us and has been for years. We're looking for a butterfly collector. Remind you of anyone?'

I swallowed awkwardly. Surely Keith wasn't involved in this deadly drama? As if on cue, Keith Giffen entered from the kitchen area behind Warren, still wearing his overcoat, saw us and began to approach.

Swivelling his head to follow my gaze, Warren noticed him as well. Keith walked briskly towards us and greeted me with a cheerful word, resting his hand on my shoulder. Warren wasn't best pleased by the unwanted interruption.

'Excuse me,' I said, easing the tension. 'This is Keith Giffen, my friend. He owns this colourful establishment.'

Warren's demeanour changed to that of conciliation. He stood, reaching out his hand to shake Keith's.

'G'day, Keith. Pleased to meet you. Beautiful place you have here.'

I hadn't introduced Warren as I guessed Keith would realise who he was. The accent was a dead giveaway.

'An Aussie?' Keith said. Suddenly, Keith winced in pain. Warren was crushing his hand. His lips were pursed, eyes narrowed.

'Warren!' At the mention of Warren's

name, Keith's eyes opened wide, the colour draining from his face.

'There's no need, Cindy. Keith and I are old buddies, aren't we, mate?' He opened his hand. Warren continued, clasping his brawny hand on the restaurateur's shoulder.

'Sorry about the hand, mate. Still, no bones broken this time and it was just a bit of fun, right? No harm done? That's what you used to say, right, me old buddy? No harm done.'

Keith grimaced, managing a weak smile.

'Yes, Warren. Certainly. Like you say, no harm done.'

'Now. If you don't mind. Cindy and I are having a private chat whilst we enjoy this rather delicious meal. You did say it was free, didn't you? For old times' sake?'

'Yes, Warren. Whatever you want!'

He was terrified!

Keith was my friend. Warren was well out of line and I was just about to stand and leave in disgust. Warren wasn't finished, though.

'One query before you leave us, if I may, Keith?' The proprietor seemed uneasy as Warren opened the lunchbox with the dead butterfly.

'Can you please identify this specimen for us, being such an enthusiastic Lepidoptera lover and all?'

Keith's eyes brightened. He was being treated as an expert by this man who had just humiliated him. Perhaps Warren wasn't such a bad person after all.

'It's beautiful, isn't it? An Adonis Blue. I used to have one years ago in my butterfly house. May I please have it — when you're finished with it, of course?'

Warren turned to me and smiled.

'Yeah. Why not? It's not as though we'll need it much longer, eh Cindy?'

With that, Keith thanked Warren before beating a hasty retreat to his kitchen area. Warren grinned smugly at me.

'My appetite has suddenly returned, Cindy. I'd call that a result, wouldn't you? And the food's free.'

He tucked into his ciabatta again,

relishing every mouthful. My mind was somersaulting in confusion.

Had Keith virtually confirmed that he was involved in poor diabetic William Lockstone's abduction and subsequent death? My friend — a criminal? But then my anger rose at the way Warren had crushed Keith's hand and humiliated him.

'Why did you do that to Keith, Warren? I didn't think the sweet boy I knew was a bully.'

I was fuming as he calmly ate his lunch while mine remained virtually untouched.

Then Warren glanced up, almost amused by my anger at him. He put his knife and fork down once more and reached across to take my hand in his as gently and lovingly as he always did.

I wasn't being placated that easily.

'How could you, Warren? You almost broke his hand with that grip of yours.'

His sincere, quiet reply cut through my anger like a knife.

'What? Like he broke mine, Cindy?'

I stared at the back of his hand, the scars from the operations still visible. He'd always been vague about what happened to shatter some of his carpel bones, forcing him to endure months of pain while he recuperated. Being determined to not give up, he'd learned to write with his left hand and was proud of his ambidexterity.

'He did that? I never suspected. He was always so thoughtful with me.'

Warren began eating again and urged me to do so. I did. After all, if Keith were involved in the death of William Lockstone, then chances were that The Kaleidoscope would soon be another empty building.

Warren explained that like Shania, Keith was a duplicitous so-and-so, a thug to Warren and a caring friend to me.

Warren apologised for his actions upsetting me. With his late maturity giving him the muscles and strength that he never had in school, he could not resist the opportunity to hurt Keith once he realised who he was.

We finished our meals without rushing and when the attractive young waitress suggested that desserts were also compliments of the management, we took pleasure in partaking of the most expensive ones on the trolley. Warren had kept an eye on them, ensuring that Keith didn't tamper with them.

'Are you going to arrest him? Keith, I mean,' I wondered.

'Me? No. I'm on hols, remember? Just seeing my family.' Warren gave me a cheeky wink. He wanted to stay undercover, at least for the present.

'In any case, I need to verify a few facts about Mr Giffen. As I recall, his family were stony broke when he was at school. How did they afford this restaurant? Ransom money, perhaps?'

He had a valid point. I decided to relate the donation of that fifty-pound note to our shop's chosen charity. Once I explained that it was for diabetes research, we both reached the same conclusion.

We left The Kaleidoscope to go our

separate ways, Warren to advise my father of developments and me to my shop. Naturally, I'd keep our suspicions and conclusions about Keith's family complicity a secret. We'd skirted around the subject of what happened next for us but we needed to face the future. Outside in the weak December sun, we stopped under the glass Victorian canopy over the footpath. Warren took charge.

'Are you and Amber free to have tea with me and my grandparents tonight, Cindy? They genuinely want to see you and clear the air, too.'

'No problem at all. What about you, Warren? I'm guessing you still have feelings for me but honestly, I'm not ready for any romance. Jimmy hurt me and that was my fault as much as his. I can't trust myself to make decisions about my future as I have to think of Amber, too.'

He grinned.

'It's a meal, Cindy. That's it. Besides, you're not the only one who's moved on with your life since school. I'm a detective in the New South Wales Police, I have a successful career and I have a special lady in my life who has sadly had to stay in Australia.

'Remember you did ask if I were married? I'm not but I do spend most of my spare time with her. Her name's Kaitlyn. I'll show you some pictures of her later on.'

I'd put my foot in it big time, suggesting that he was infatuated with me when all this time he had a girlfriend back home. How stupid of me. He was bright, handsome and all of those adjectives that supposedly described the perfect man. Why on earth would he be interested in me?

I forced my grimace into a half-smile. It was hard.

'Tonight then, Cindy. I'll collect you and Amber at — shall we say seven?'

'But you don't know where I live.'

He chuckled, tapping his nose.

'I'm a detective, remember? Give me some credit to uncover your secrets and if that fails, I'll ask your dad.'

As he walked off, I turned to stare after

him, feeling a mixture of emotions.

'Lucky Kaitlyn,' I said, under my breath, as I dabbed my eyes.

Finally, I sighed, pulled my collar up and hurried back towards the shop. Between us, we'd cracked that original kidnap case so I should have been pleased. It was almost Christmas and the shop was doing well. I should have been happy but I felt quite apprehensive about Friday night.

I saw it in my mind's eye already. We'd be sitting in front of the telly and Warren would be blue-toothing his phone photographs on to the big screen for me to see. Yeah. Photographs of Warren and perfect Kaitlyn with her tan and sun-bleached hair and perfect teeth.

12

A little before three, Dad rang the shop. Hannah answered and passed me the receiver.

'Just thought that you'd like to hear it from me, petal. We're set to arrest Keith Giffen in around fifteen minutes. High profile op.'

I was puzzled.

'Why tell me, Dad?'

'In case you wanted a front-row seat. Once you and Warren made the connection, the evidence fell into place like a line of dominos. Keith's father, Thaddeus, went from broke to well off overnight around the date William Lockstone was snatched. That's when he made an offer on the restaurant.

'Of course, the sale took a while to go through which is why we missed someone splashing out cash then. He drip-fed cash into various accounts before using them for the purchase. After that he exaggerated the takings, laundering more money as profit from The Kaleidoscope over all this time.

'Our fraud squad spotted the technique as soon as Warren suggested him as a suspect. Gold stars to you two.'

It explained a lot. Mrs Giffen was now one of those women who was famous for her elaborate lifestyle and parties.

'Any hint on Bart's whereabouts as yet?'

'Sadly not, Cindy. We're praying that either this Keith Giffen chap or his father will crack under pressure. Keith was sixteen at the time so hardly the brains behind the abduction. We have a team set to pounce on Daddy Giffen at his home and another simultaneously arresting Keith. It's hush-hush so don't tell anyone.'

I promised that I wouldn't. Hannah and Georgia had been busy with sales but guessed that I was elated when I approached them grinning like the Cheshire Cat.

'I'm guessing that Dad had good news

about Bart,' Georgia suggested.

'Well, a breakthrough. Do you mind if I go watch? I can't give details. Not yet anyway?'

'Fine, Cindy,' Georgia told me, sharing my joy. Hannah excused herself to assist a woman at the far end of the shop.

'Just please tell us what happens, Cindy. I hope they rescue Bart Travis soon. It must be so terrible for him being locked up in the dark all of this time.'

Despite all the evidence suggesting that Keith was involved, I felt guilty. He'd been my friend and I wasn't able to switch my emotions off.

When Hannah returned, I asked about the customer. She said the lady wanted to check if we offered a fifty per cent discount to locals. We found that quite amusing. The cheek of some people.

It was time for me to take my leave to witness Keith's arrest. I was more concerned about his long-deceased victim getting justice at last. I had many unanswered questions and it had been five days since Bart went missing.

Outside, the steady drizzle prompted me to shelter under my umbrella. One of the good things about life in Southport was the absence of the snow flurries and thick mounds of the horrible white stuff throughout winter.

For that reason, I grudgingly tolerated the rain today as I carefully hurried along the pedestrian precinct and through the Cambridge Arcade towards Lord Street. The Kaleidoscope wasn't that far.

By the time I arrived, three marked police cars were silently parked up outside with officers directing traffic and pedestrians away from the restaurant. Doubtless they wanted the computers inside to examine them, both for financial irregularities and emails regarding Bart Travis.

My father orchestrated the actions of plain clothes and uniformed officers. He was certainly anxious to achieve maximum publicity, as two camera crews from nearby networks were present and filming the event. The evidence against Keith must have been irrefutable.

I kept my umbrella up, grateful that the dreaded Southport winds from the sea were taking a day off. Simultaneously raids would be made on Keith's restaurant and his family home in Birkdale. Theirs was the same home with Keith's butterfly collection housed in a large heated greenhouse.

We presumed that William Lockstone had probably died there from hyperglycemia or too much sugar in his blood, damaging his heart It was the sole explanation for the Alpine Blue butterfly specimen being found in his clothing.

'What's happening?' one elderly bystander asked a friend of hers. I collapsed my umbrella. The rain had ceased, an icy blue sky replacing the pewter grey clouds as they moved inland.

'It looks like they're interested in that butterfly eating joint. Maybe food poisoning or summat? See . . . the owner is coming out now in handcuffs,' her male companion suggested.

He was correct. Keith Giffen was not a happy bunny. He tried to shield his face from the cameras as my father stepped forward to caution him.

With a scowl, Keith's eyes narrowed as he scanned the crowd before fixing his gaze on me. I heard a phone ringing. Bob Lind's 'The Elusive Butterfly' if my Sixties song memory served me right. Keith made a move to answer it but, with his hands constrained, was unable to get it. Instead, a detective retrieved it from his inside coat pocket.

'Hey. Give that back. It's mine.'

The detective ignored Keith completely, opened it and showed a text to my father. He scowled.

'Seems like someone is warning you to make a run for it, Keith. 'The police are making arrests. Exit strategy, son, Make it fast.'

'How sweet. Would you like me to type your reply? Along the lines of 'Too late, Pater, dearest. I've been nicked'?'

Keith was fuming.

'You have no idea who you're dealing with here. You'll be sorry.'

'I'm already sorry, Butterfly-Boy. Sorry

for the death of the man you imprisoned and let die years ago. Sorry for his parents who paid the ransom, expecting to save their son.

'Sorry for Bart Travis who you and your family probably abducted as well and sorry for all of these people gathered here having to see that dreadful pink faux fur you're wearing. Didn't your mater tell you? Pink is so last year.'

Keith reacted more to the insult of his fashion sense than the other accusations. He sought an escape from this continuing public humiliation. He found it in the crowd.

'Ah, there you are. Come to gloat, have you? It was you, Cindy Powers. Or shall I call you Judas? Telling tales to Daddy Dearest. You're the one responsible for this travesty of justice.'

This was the Keith that had bullied Warren in school. My flamboyant friend's true dark side had now emerged. Bravely, I stood up to his vindictive words as he continued. Sergeant Uncle Gerry Hawkins moved to silence Keith but my father stopped him with a quiet word, eager to let the angry insults continue.

After all, Keith had been cautioned. Any words he said could be used against him and, at this moment, Keith had loads to say.

With a start, I realised that the camera crews weren't media at all. I recognised officers dressed as reporters in an elaborate charade. Dad had orchestrated my presence here to goad Keith's anger.

The tirade meant nothing to me. I tolerated Jimmy's temper for years and had learned to rise above it, responding to his anger with quiet indifference. My father was aware of this. He was using me and was confident that I'd ignore Keith's wrath. Dad winked at me.

'Don't you dare blame me, Keith Giffen. You and your family killed William Lockstone ten years ago and kept the ransom.' My voice was loud but controlled.

His temper flared.

'No, I didn't you, pathetic woman.

He died. Natural causes. Not my fault if his body didn't work properly. It was an accident. He was confused and thirsty, complaining of a headache. He told me he needed that insulin stuff but because he was confused, I looked it up. Anyway, I gave him sugar like it said I was supposed to.'

He was incandescent, shaking his cuffed hands at me as I struggled to process what he'd just admitted. Moreover, his confession was on videotape in glorious colour and stereo sound. At last, he realised his schoolboy error about talking too much and calmed down.

A few police and my father understood the shocking implications of Keith's admission but it fell to me to say it aloud. Even I knew the difference between hypo and hyperglycaemia.

Hyperglycaemia was having too much sugar; hypoglycaemia was too little sugar in the blood.

William Lockstone was suffering from a lack of insulin and a lot of excess sugar. So, what had Keith done? Exactly the worst thing possible.

Despite his denials, Keith had effectively murdered William.

As calmly and as simply as I could, I explained Keith's error to him.

'I . . . I never realised. I'm sorry. So, so sorry.' He turned to each officer then my father and finally me. 'I never meant to do that. Honest. But I did . . . I killed him.' Then he sank to the rain-drenched footpath sobbing uncontrollably. My father led me away as Keith was helped into the rear seat of a marked patrol car.

He wasn't finished though. He pushed the officer back and addressed me defiantly as if he'd garnered a final burst of his arrogant Hyde persona.

'You're a witch, Cindy Powers. Shania always says that about you. Your reaction to those pamphlets back in school did exactly what we hoped. Screwed your precious daddy's mind up good and proper.

I retorted with a sedate smugness.

'Yet here we are, Keith. You and me. But you confessed to murder. You're finished.'

Any semblance of that defiance faded as the truth struck home. He was going to prison for a long time. Even now, The Kaleidoscope was being meticulously torn apart by forensics and IT experts. My father came to embrace me.

'You did well, sweetheart. Warren couldn't be here as we need to maintain his cover.'

At that moment, a woman detective, whose name I didn't recall, approached us.

'Sorry boss. Bad news. We had the house under distant surveillance but the drone's camera was down for a few minutes due to the weather. When the second team hit old man Giffen's place, he'd flown the coop. We arrested the wife as arranged but Thaddeus Giffen isn't there. His car's gone, too.'

Dad suppressed his displeasure, clenching his fists in frustration rather than berating the bearer of bad news.

'But he was there. Bravo team saw him in the garden . . . No matter. Put out an

APB and get on to the ANPR team to find his car, Jasmine. He can't have got far.'

I managed to recall the oft-used acronyms from telly police shows; All Points Bulletin and Automatic Number Plate Recognition.

'Do you believe he was tipped off, boss?'

'Almost certainly.'

The suggestion was there but unspoken. Thaddeus Giffen had a mole in the local police.

13

Warren collected us as arranged. He found where we lived easily, being in his modest words, a very clever detective. Amber opened our front door to him once I buzzed him through the downstairs security entrance.

Her pleasure at seeing him again was enhanced when he passed her 'a pressie from the other side of the world'.

Prising the lid off with her tiny fingers was hard but she managed it, staring at the stuffed toy inside. As she lifted it to examine it more closely, Amber tipped her head to the side, her hair flopping onto the gift momentarily.

Warren bent over to explain.

'She's an Australian teddy bear, Amber. She's called a koala. And look, she has a baby koala in her pouch just like real ones do.'

She hugged the toy close and then straightened the ears bent from being stuffed into the shoe box.

'Well. The baby can be Goldie and the Mummy can be Koka.'

Warren and I exchanged looks then both smiled as we understood.

Warren ruffled her hair but, for once, she didn't object.

'Koka Koala? Just like the drink. Wow. That's very clever, Amber. You have the same sense of humour as your mummy.'

I relaxed. Warren and I had been so close during our school days but any hopes of rekindling our special bond had been scuppered by the elephant in the room, a pretty pachyderm named Kaitlyn.

Leaving the packaging on the table, we locked up and stepped into the lift. Being so close, I was aware of his musky aftershave.

We stepped from the lift on the ground floor. Devina was there peering intently out the front door. She jumped as I called her name.

Brief introductions over, she greeted me and Warren, explaining that a man was lurking over the street. She'd spotted him an hour before from her apartment facing the front and had come downstairs to keep a better eye on him.

'She's right, Cindy. I noticed him in the shadows when I parked outside. Should I have a discreet word?'

Although Devina said nothing, her unease was clear. She was more scared than I'd seen before. Given her comments about family, particularly her father, I chose to make an executive decision, thanking Warren for his offer and asking for his intervention.

The moment he exited our apartment building and headed across the road, our shadowy observer made his move, walking briskly around the corner, down Gordon Street. Warren stopped.

As for the identity of the unsavoury character, I gathered from Devina's expression that her fears were confirmed. His face was clear to see under the street light he passed under before slinking off.

'Was that . . . ?'

'Yeah. My not-so-loving father.' Her

voice was filled with contempt.

'Should I cancel dinner and stay with you?'

She cheered up, although I suspected it was purely for my benefit.

'No way, Cindy. You're only a phone call away and we have great security.'

Warren's grandparents made us most welcome when Amber and I arrived. The rudeness of that phone call earlier in the week was now fully resolved and forgotten. The deviousness of Shania framing Warren all those years before was out in the open for all to see. The reunion was quite emotional with tears and hugs and regrets of words said in the heat of moments long gone.

From the kitchen, I heard Amber's voice chatting to Colin as they prepared the final touches for tonight's meal. A man in the kitchen? How times were changing. Neither my father nor Jimmy bothered with such domestic pursuits.

I addressed Warren mainly as he was the policeman involved in the case and he'd familiarised his grandparents with developments each evening.

'When Keith was in full rant mode on the Lord Street, he shouted something like 'Shania says you're a witch'. Not 'said' — 'says'. That implies that they're in touch at present.'

He sat forward.

'So she may be involved in the kidnaps also? And Jimmy? A group of school kids back then, being manipulated by Keith's father.'

That made sense to me. Dad was always puzzled by the ineptitude of some of the kidnappers ten years ago. Who would have suspected teenagers being involved? Was Shania the one diverting my father's attention from the case as she did then? Definitely worth further inquiries.

Warren read my mind.

'I'll track her down, Cindy. On the quiet, though. Your father informed me of that slanging match with my old mate, Keith. Showed me the whole thing on video, in fact. You gave as good as you got and forced him to confess to manslaughter. I'm proud of you.'

Warren's admiration was welcome, yet did I desire more than that? Another Christmas kiss?

'Earth to Cindy? Are you receiving? Over.' Brenda gently nudged me.

I shook my head. Daydreaming about an unrequited romance?

'Sorry. Away with the fairies. Any news about Thaddeus Giffen?'

Warren shook his head, frustrated.

'None. He was tipped off, though; text from a burner phone sent minutes before twelve. He texted Keith in turn, warning him but, as you know, he was too late.

Thaddeus left his missus to cope with the police, but we're unsure about her involvement. Not to be unkind but Mrs Giffen probably reckons that a polar cap is a type of hat. Thaddeus Giffen told everyone he could that he never married her for her brains.'

Is that why The Elsewhens had signalled me out this Christmas? To expose the evil team of kidnappers? If so, I was doing OK. Keith was in custody and his father was next on the to-do list of criminal catching.

But what about Bart? He'd been snatched five days earlier from the coastal path, presumably bundled into a vehicle of some type. Since then, the police had received regular updates showing him alive and well in a darkened, nondescript room.

Taking their time (which was unusual), the kidnappers demanded two million in unmarked non-sequential used notes. That was rather old-fashioned of them given the more modern methods of money transfers via untraceable banks in tax havens.

As Warren and my dad intimated, we were dealing with cool but unsophisticated villains, seemingly repeating the same crime from ten years before on the principle that it worked first time around.

The ransom drop-off was scheduled for Sunday at a place and time to be advised. Bart would then be returned unharmed. Either the police located Bart beforehand from questioning Keith, or the ransom would be paid. The chances of tracing the victim by other means were very slim.

Regarding the promised photos of Kaitlyn, I didn't press the issue. With any luck, he'd forget to show them and I'd avoid the humiliation.

No. Best not to mention the K-word at all. Warren and my family were friends again and whatever else there might have been with Warren and myself was just another train-wreck casualty in my love life.

Amber entered the room. We stopped our conversation as she announced very politely, 'Ladies and gentlemen. Dinner is served.'

Colin applauded her rehearsed lines as we all moved to the dining room with its resplendent Christmas tree in the alcove by the mahogany fireplace.

The cottage pie with winter vegetables was excellent. Bored with retirement, Colin had assumed some responsibilities for cooking and baking in the household. After we finished the three-course meal, he brought in his first attempt at a Christmas cake. I loosened my belt. So much for my pre-Christmas diet.

As we cleared the dishes, Brenda called to Warren.

'Before you forget, Warren, fetch those photos of you and Kaitlyn, please. Your iPad should be charged by now, I'm sure. We're all looking forward to seeing this new love of yours.'

'Oh. She's not new, Gran. We've been an item around Sydney for about a year. You don't mind seeing my home movies and photos, do you, Cindy? Even though you never, in your own words, felt anything romantic about me.'

Rats and double rats. I forced myself to keep a straight face. He was trying to put me on the spot and doing a fairly good job, too.

'I love home movies, Warren. And I'm keen to see how beautiful Kaitlyn is. Not, as you say, that your relationship is any of my concern. Shall we start or wait for the popcorn to arrive?'

Warren returned with his digital photo

library and connected it to the smart television. We made ourselves comfortable, Amber showing no signs of sleepiness. She was snuggled up next to me.

'Everyone ready? Cindy Powers? You look a little green in the face. Jealousy, perhaps?'

I shifted uncomfortably under everyone's gaze.

'Hardly. As for my skin colour, I'm sure it's a reflection off that dreadful shirt of yours. I thought that lime green clothing was more suited to children?'

We relaxed into our respective cushions, all glued to the screen. I hoped they'd dim the lights so that my gnashing of teeth wasn't that obvious, but no. The lights stayed on. The big-screen photo showed one of those perfect Sydney beaches on a naturally perfect sunny day.

'This was our first time out together,' Warren announced proudly.

The scene was in a parking lot with cars, SUVs and cycles in the foreground then lawn and glistening, golden sands leading down to the breaking surf. Scattered dots of people were on the beach, a stunning blonde in a red bikini waving to the camera.

She had sunglasses on and one of those figures that was just like the rest of the scene . . . nauseatingly perfect.

'Isn't she beautiful, Mummy?'

'Et tu, Amber?' I sighed. I certainly didn't feel inclined to respond.

Amber turned to me questioningly.

'Yes, sweetheart. Absolutely beautiful. Warren is so lucky.'

It was going to be along, painful night.

14

Prior to dinner, when Warren went to give Amber a hand setting the table, Brenda mentioned that she and Colin had yet to see the mysterious latest love in Warren's life. Naturally, they'd kept in touch during the ensuing years since he and their daughter returned to warmer climes. They'd followed his career with interest and were overjoyed when he told them of his return to the area on secondment.

'We wondered if his choice of police authority in England might have some connection to you as well as us but, with Kaitlyn on the scene, it seems not.'

'You told him about me and Jimmy getting divorced?'

Brenda shrugged. She hadn't changed that much from the caring woman who'd been like my second mum in school. More silver hairs, a few extra pounds since her health meant she'd cut back on her love of walking along the coastal trails and gardening.

'Yes, Cindy. Word gets around in Southport, as you well know. In many ways, we're like a village rather than a town. Your mum and I still have the same friends on Facebook.

'We never interacted after ... you know, but I'd see her posts from time to time. Reading between the lines, you had a rough time with that Jimmy chap. He dealt with him on the bench. Community order, if memory serves me right.'

That was a revelation.

'I never realised. Then again, his and Shania's decade of deception as lovers had fooled me. I must be the dumbest dumb bunny on the planet.'

The conversation finished then as Warren re-entered the room. Having heard my last few words, Warren closed the conversation down flat with a wink and a typically irreverent comment.

'You? A dumb bunny? No way, Cindy. But I do reckon you have the cutest cotton tail.'

He clicked the photos through, one by one. More from different angles, some with him posing in the parking area with and without a shirt. Not that he had one of those six-pack tummies but the muscles and supposed fitness regime were apparent.

'Where's Kaitlyn? Is she taking the pictures? I can't see her.' We'd watched over a dozen shots from all angles in that parking lot, but the stunning lady in Warren's life was conspicuous by her absence.

'She's there, Mummy. The red one?' Amber said.

Warren coughed discreetly, hand over mouth to conceal a grin perhaps. A titter escaped the lips of the others. Were they laughing at me?

Then I realised. Standing with arms folded so I blocked the view of the television, I narrowed my gaze. I'd been played. 'Excuse me, Detective Ross. This Kaitlyn you go everywhere with. She's not a motorcycle, is she?'

He burst out laughing.

'Too right . . . Kaitlyn Kawasaki. The sweetest bike I've ridden. 1983 GPz 1100c. Fully reconditioned. Don't you just love those lines, Cindy?'

What could I say?

'I never pegged you as Mad Max, Warren. But there you go. Don't tell me that you were all a party to this little joke?'

Warren's laughter changed to a subdued chuckle.

'Afraid so, Cindy. Even little Amber, bless her, keeping the secret and all. She did very well, too.'

The truth was that I was beaten. It was time to try another approach.

'So, Detective Warren . . . May I assume that you have no romantic feelings for anyone?'

His response worried me and intrigued me at the same time.

'Only you, my dearest Cindy. Only you.'

The evening that I'd dreaded was now memorable in quite a different way. Warren loved me and me alone. Although

I wasn't ready to reciprocate at the moment, his long standing desire to be a part of my life was swaying my feelings towards him.

The day had been a rollercoaster of events and emotions. I was exhausted.

As Warren pulled into the front parking area, I nonchalantly scanned the shadows for Devina's father. He wasn't to be seen.

'Good news for your friend,' Warren said, reading my mind. He'd checked the area out too as he drove in.

'If Devina wishes to call the station later tomorrow morning, I'll have informed them of what happened. I gather they take a dim view of stalking around Southport.' To virtually everyone, he was a visitor for a few weeks and he was quite right to distance himself from reporting stalking as questions might be asked.

I doubted that Keith suspected that Warren was undercover and we needed to maintain that deception for the foreseeable.

Amber had managed to stay awake whilst at Brenda's and Colin's but had, in the short drive home, succumbed to nodding off on the back seat.

'No dramas, Cindy. I'll carry her up. Shame to wake her.'

I appreciated his kindness, wondering if the two of us might continue the night upstairs with mugs of coffee. Laying Amber on her bed, he politely declined my invitation.

'Early start tomorrow. We're planning to search abandoned farmhouses and isolated buildings. One of the proof-of-life photos had what appeared to be hay or straw visible.'

We turned off the main light in Amber's room, leaving the night light's subtle glow to illuminate her cuddling Koka Koala and her proper Teddy. He reached to take my hand before deciding that a cheek kiss goodbye was more appropriate. If he'd moved his lips to mine, I wouldn't have objected. Nevertheless, his breath grazing my skin felt sensual.

'Cindy. You did well today — with Keith, I mean. All thanks to that butterfly from the past. Don't suppose you've had any further Elsewhere visions?'

'Elsewhen. And no, I can't switch them on and off. I just wish you had caught Thaddeus as well as his son.'

'As do I. Keith has clammed up. He's already confessed to the murder. In any case, we had a victory today. As a copper, you learn to enjoy whatever successes you achieve. As they say, tomorrow's another day.'

I was reluctant to say farewell. Tonight had taught me that I had feelings for him that extended way past friendship. Why couldn't I move past my marriage and the pain it still caused? More importantly, would Warren wait for me?

After he closed the door, I made sure it was locked. The presence of Devina's father loitering outside worried me.

My diaries were on the bedside table, beckoning me to read them again. I'd missed whatever was there the first time around. This time I needed to concentrate on every word to check, once and for all, whether any inkling about the criminals was there to throw light on the current situation.

Fourteen pages into the second diary, I found the first hint. Another fifteen pages in, my suspicions were confirmed. It had been worth sifting through the mind-numbing drivel about music, school and who was in love with whom.

Shania, my erstwhile bestie, confidant and role model for all that was cool in the world, had a much younger cousin at a neighbouring school. Shania introduced us once when we met at a dance in Ainsdale. Not that I recalled her face at all. Were it not for my diary, her name would be a blur, too.

'Gotcha!' I muttered.

My first breakthrough was the cousin's name, the second was that she was close friends with the Giffen family. Was she the mole who warned Thaddeus that he was about to be arrested earlier today? As I switched off my bedside lamp, I snuggled down under the duvet, resolved that tomorrow Cindy Powers would do her best work to unearth the truth about her. Once that was done, she and I would have a cosy chat.

* * *

I arrived early at The Love Affair, turned off the alarm and entered the store. I felt as if someone were watching and saw a silhouette in the shadows. Switching on the light, I breathed a sigh of relief.

'Sorry, Cupid,' I apologised to the statue.

Watching the security video from the interior, I feared what I'd discover as it meant betrayal by someone I considered a friend. That she'd manipulated me to ingratiate herself into my life was sickening. She was a spy.

The connection to my father and my history were the reasons — good old gullible Lucinda Powers. This all happened months before the abduction as part of a long-term scheme.

I stood up, ready to engage in my

own Christmas pantomime. It was time for payback. Our butter-wouldn't-melt teenage assistant, Hannah McCann, didn't stand a chance.

15

By the time Georgia and Hannah arrived for what promised to be a hectic Saturday, I'd calmed down. Our surveillance recordings revealed that, just before noon yesterday, Hannah went to assist a customer at the far end of the shop.

Dealing with the lady quickly, she'd moved out of our line of sight but not the camera view. She texted somebody. My money on was Thaddeus Giffen, based on her furtive and secretive behaviour.

Not that I'd said anything about the raid after Dad rang but she might have overheard us and his side of the conversation. Shania referred to her as Big Ears and my younger self had recorded that description in my diary entry. I mentioned that wherever I was heading was nearby. Big Ears probably realised what was happening and warned Keith's father.

I wondered if Hannah was aware of

where Bart was being held. Upon reflection, probably not. But if my plan worked, the police might use her to reveal his hiding place.

Hannah and Georgia approached me at the cash desk, both dusting specks of snow from their hats and coats.

I stared at Hannah, more particularly her neck. 'Just a smidge. Is something wrong, Cindy?' she asked self-consciously. 'Just admiring that choker you're wearing. Is it new?' She fingered it proudly.

'Yeah. My boyfriend gave it me as a one-week to Christmas present. Said the blue matches my eyes. Do you like it?'

'It suits you. Very chic. New perfume, as well? Penhaligon's Halfeti if I'm not mistaken.'

She blushed.

'Yes. How did you guess? Do you have the same?'

I laughed, nonchalantly. 'Me? No. Out of my price range. You're very lucky to have such a rich guy in your life.'

'Yeah. Guess I am. Shall I open up

now?'

'Yes, please. Can't keep the customers waiting, can we?' I replied. 'Who fancies a cuppa?'

Hannah and Georgia both said yes. I decided not to enlighten my sister about Hannah's duplicitous nature until my scheme to convincingly expose our assistant was complete.

In the kitchenette, I tipped out the milk from the plastic bottle, washing it down the sink. Returning to my companions, I held the bottle aloft, and pulled a face.

'Sorry, guys. Milk's off. Tipped it out. I'll nip round to Tescos. Grab some mince pies, as well. That OK with you, Hannah?'

She giggled.

'Mince pies? Need you ask, Cindy? You know they're my kryptonite.'

The snowflakes were coming down more heavily as I hurried along Chapel Street's pedestrian way, deciding not to use the awning along the side with the railway station entrance.

All the other shoppers were crowding

under them, bumping into one another because their heads were bent low.

I dialled Dad's mobile.

'I'm busy, love. Better be quick,' was his brusque response.

'The mole, Dad. I'm certain that it's Hannah. Yes, Hannah McCann from the shop. She messaged a number at midday and five minutes later, Thaddeus Giffen is on the run. I'm texting you her number. Check her call history.

'If it confirms my suspicions, come around to the shop. And bring Warren. It's time to let the Aussie cat out of the bag.'

He agreed. Warren's role undercover had run its course. We continued to discuss options as I grabbed the milk and mince pies, paid at a self-service checkout and made my way back.

By now, the snow was sticking. Almost slipping twice, I slowed down as the mini-blizzard stopped as quickly as it began. Good. This was the second last Saturday before Christmas. We needed shoppers out. Hopefully, the weather was clearing up for the rest of the day.

'Watch yourself, petal,' he warned. His words warmed my whole body. Any trust issues we'd had in the past were long since resolved.

'I will Dad. Hopefully, see you soon. If everything goes to plan, we'd find Bart Travis before nightfall.'

Three hours later, my father arrived on the pretext of taking a break to admire our enterprise. He had never been inside The Love Affair since we opened.

Hannah was curious. Such behaviour at this crucial juncture was completely out of character. Wasn't the ransom to be paid this weekend? Although working at the till, her attention was focused on me, Georgia, Dad and our conversations.

He eyed the displays and décor slowly, adding titbits of approving comments when he spied an object which took his fancy.

'This is a credit to you both, ladies. Together, you've achieved something magnificent. What's even better is that the two of you aren't scrapping like cats and dogs like you did as teenagers. The number of occasions your mum or I had to break up a fight . . .'

We both chuckled.

Dad peered over my shoulder to the snowy street outside. That prompted me to swivel around. Georgia noticed them also, beating me in her demands for answers.

'Dad. Are those police officers standing guard outside our shop? No offence, but not a great incentive to visit us. Why are they there?'

Our father did his best to allay Georgia's genuine agitation.

The few customers browsing were watching us with interest.

Dad gathered us in a huddle so as not to be overheard by all and sundry. Hannah was close enough to hear his more subdued explanation.

'They're here temporarily. I'm waiting for . . . Ah, there he is. Honestly. Some people have no concept of being on time.'

As the huge newcomer wandered up slowly, watching his footing, he addressed the two uniformed police, they nodded before moving off to patrol the busy shopping precinct. He entered the shop, unwrapping the long scarf and gradually revealing his face.

Warren was done up like a giant wombat with multiple layers of coats and jumpers making him look rather comical. Moreover, he was waddling instead of walking.

'Sorry, I'm late, guv. What do you want me to do? Babysit?'

Georgia played her part beautifully. I guessed she react like this, always wishing to be in control. Not that I'd appraised her of what Dad and I planned. Her spontaneity and irritation were perfect.

All the time, Hannah watched from the corner of her eye, intrigued by the proceedings. Just then, twin sisters approached her at the till, presents clutched in their eager hands. They were early twenties, identical and usually frequented our Love Affair on Saturdays.

I waved to them before being immersed again in the family drama that now included Warren. Georgia's eyes showed confusion.

'Why are you calling our father Guv? Don't tell me you're police as well?'

'Too right, I'm a copper, young lady. Undercover. Someone has to keep an eye on you lot, considering what happened.' He wasn't pleased and, from his narrowed eyes, he blamed our father.

Dad feigned indignation, raising his voice.

'Watch your tongue, Detective. It wasn't my fault that he escaped.'

Warren shrugged.

'Just the way I see it there's not much point proving this Keith bloke's one of the kidnappers if he's on the loose again. Do you have revolving doors on your cells?'

Dad scowled.

'He was being transferred to Crosby Police Station. An unfortunate RTA. He made a break for it when the van crashed.'

Georgia gasped.

'The butterfly man's escaped? Are we

in danger, Warren?'

Warren spoke to reassure her.

'Not with me, around, Georgia. I'll blend in; keep an eye on things in the shop.'

My sister wasn't impressed.

Warren tried to reassure her.

'I can help out with putting your expensive pressies on shelves, if you want. Used to lend a hand in my mum's shop near Coogee Beach.

'One thing I learnt was how to tie a mean bow with ribbon. Yeah. Maybe I can be an undercover assistant, helping with the gift wrapping and other fancy stuff. Yeah. Standing by that electric radiator will suit me peachy. No worries.'

He went to the kitchenette to remove his multiple layers of clothing. Georgia stared in astonishment and stormed off, declaring that she was going for lunch and a very large glass of wine.

Meanwhile, our father decided that he'd overstayed his brief visit. That meant I was alone with the twins, waiting by the counter expectantly. Even Hannah had vanished.

I smiled my best apologetic smile as I hurried to them.

'Sorry about the wait, ladies. How may I assist you?'

'We wanted these gift-wrapped, please. And to buy them, naturally. Your girl Friday went to fetch another roll for your payment machine. But we're not in a rush. Anything but. The entertainment here is first class.'

I fumbled in the drawer under the desk where we shoved all sorts and retrieved a roll for our electronic transaction machine.

As promised, Warren began with his ribbon thing, adeptly doing an excellent job.

The twins then sashayed from The Love Affair.

Hannah startled us as she appeared from one of the storerooms, a box of new till receipts in her hand.

'Where are they going? They haven't paid, yet,' she said.

I reassured her that they had,

explaining that there were usually spare rolls in the miscellaneous drawer. After that, I resumed my wanders around the store, assisting customers whilst Hannah and Warren worked in tandem, collecting payments and wrapping. Georgia hadn't returned but that suited me fine. Time for the next part of my scheme.

Loads of shoppers were wandering the streets of Southport. The three of us were run off our feet with customers. Hannah bemoaned Georgia's extended absence because, handsome as he was, our resident detective was useless as a sales assistant. Tying bows was his one forte and it simply wasn't enough.

At two thirty-five he noticed the time on our clock. He excused himself in the middle of a rush to the cashier's desk, saying he was late for an important conference phone call with headquarters.

Moments later, he was back.

'My phone must be in the car. May I borrow yours, Cindy?'

'Sure. But it's playing up. The battery keeps going flat for no reason. Let me check it?' I did, in between wrapping a small watch for an older guy.

'Darn. No good. It's flat again. What about your mobile, Hannah?' I asked.

'I really need to make this call,' Warren pleaded.

Hannah was quite flustered herself, completing a transaction whilst chatting politely with a family who were waiting.

'Phone? Sure. Here you go.' She took it from her pocket and unlocked it, too confused to recall that The Love Affair had a landline which Warren might have used whenever he wanted.

I kept her busy with other tasks until Warren returned, nodding to me. I slowed down, intent on enjoying the next few delicious minutes.

'Thanks, Hannah. For the phone, I mean,' he said.

'Good. May I have it back, please?' She held one hand out while passing a receipt to a teenager with the other.

'Nope. 'Fraid not,' Warren stated, standing resolute.

'Sorry?' Hannah said, suddenly giving

him her full attention.

'It's evidence.' At that point, Warren sighed before launching into a speech he knew by heart. Hannah remained mute, listening to the caution yet seemingly astounded to hear it being directed at her.

'Definitely gotcha,' I whispered to myself, feeling justified at our deceptions.

Hannah McCann was arrested for aiding and abetting in the unlawful imprisonment of Bart Travis. I prayed that the rest of our scheme might be as successful.

16

We were aware of those customers in the shop watching us with great interest. Any suspicion that it was a joke vanished as Warren produced folding handcuffs from his belt and fitted them on Hannah.

'I've discovered a text you sent to someone, advising him of the news about Keith escaping. I assume this message is intended for his father, a wanted criminal. You included the word 'son' next to Keith's name. Unhappily for Keith, he's still in a cell, contemplating being found guilty of murder.'

That news prompted Hannah's sweet nature to dissolve as she lashed out.

'You tricked me, you filthy piece of garbage. Keith's so sweet. He doesn't deserve to be locked away from his butterflies.'

'Like I said, he's a murderer, by his own admission. Now, where's Bart

Travis? It'll go easier on you if you tell me immediately.'

My father entered, no doubt summoned by Warren. Georgia was with him as were two uniformed officers. Georgia politely asked the browsers to leave, and she flipped the closed sign to the outside of the door and locked it. Dad must have told her everything and kept her from coming back until our deception to trap Hannah was complete.

Hannah, for her part, became passive again saying that she had no clue about Bart's whereabouts. Her role was to confound the investigation by reporting on our family. Her accusation that Warren had perused her phone messages illegally was dismissed.

'You gave him permission to use it. The conversation was recorded,' the female sergeant explained. 'In any case, we applied for your mobile's call history and have proof that you warned the same person as now about yesterday's raids.

'Units are converging on the location you sent the text to. We might not have the information as to who owns such a phone but we can trace the location to the nearest cell tower.'

Hannah wasn't convinced.

'Another lie. You lot are so good at it.'

Georgia stepped forward to have her say.

'You're the liar, Hannah. How could you? We trusted you. Was it money? Did Thaddeus Giffen promise you a few thousand pounds from the ransom?'

She sneered.

'Money? Hah! You haven't got the faintest idea, have you? And Thaddeus's not in charge. Not this ti . . .' She clammed up then.

No names but once again she'd slipped up and she realised it.

As the three police marched Hannah out the door, Georgia flipped the sign to Open again.

'What?' she said, staring at my surprised expression. 'Curious onlookers equal customers. As for you, Detective, we're short handed. I don't suppose . . . ?'

Warren hastened to collect his plethora

of cold-weather clothing.

'Sorry. I'll have to fill out Hannah's arrest documents. Besides, my fingers are aching from all that ribbon tying. Never imagined that you ladies did such hard work. Also, far too much drama in this shop for my liking. Coppers everywhere.' He grinned, pulled on his gloves and left.

'We're in trouble, big time,' Georgia observed as the crowd from outside suddenly descended on our shop. 'I don't suppose your plan to arrest our assistant could have waited till after Christmas?'

'You're right. I didn't think things through. My bad,' I replied, equally sarcastically. The line from outside was still there, filing patiently through the door. Inside we must have had twenty people already. We'd never had so many at one time and I was feeling overwhelmed. Then I spotted a lifeline as Devina entered, phone to her ear.

Frantically, I waved to attract her attention. Spotting me, she waved back but seemed oblivious to why I was gesturing.

Finally, she understood and clicked her phone off before gently pushing through the throngs already waiting to be served.

'What's going on? All those police plus your father. Surely not a shop-lifter?'

'Worse. Our assistant. I don't suppose that you're doing anything special this afternoon? We'll pay you, naturally.'

'You had me at the word 'pay', Cindy. Seriously, I would have helped anyway. Tell me what you want me to do after I get my coat off. Wow. It's manic in here.'

Georgia began to protest at my unilateral decision but I put her mind at ease.

'She's the Indian student from downstairs in my apartment block. We have tea together most nights. I trust her. And she's worked in Harrod's. I've seen photos.'

Georgia relaxed.

'I do believe you have redeemed yourself. We might survive this yet.'

Devina proved to be an angel. She was everywhere at once, replacing stock, assisting customers in their search for the perfect gift for Aunt Victoria, and her skills at wrapping left us both amazed.

We stayed open until six, much later than usual as the flow of customers continued. Finally, exhausted but elated, Devina flipped the Closed sign to the outside and locked the door.

'We'll need to restock the shelves.'

'Not tonight, Georgia. I'm bushed. I'll come in at nine tomorrow. How about you, Devina? Are you available to assist us for a few days? You were brilliant today. Saved our bacon. Oops, sorry. No offence.'

'I'm not Hindu, Cindy. Christian. Just like you. Born in London but my family are from Ponicherry where there are lots of Christians. I've just put up my Christmas tree. This is my special time of the year, too.'

I apologised for my ignorance. To be fair, she'd told me very little about herself whereas I must have bored her with too much information about me. I prayed that last night's encounter with her mysterious father had enticed her to trust me more.

Deciding to be pushier with her than I'd been already, I suggested a takeaway tonight at her apartment.

'I've never been to yours and Amber will love to see your tree. We can go up to mine when it's time for her bed. Share a taxi home. How does that sound to you, Devina?'

'Yes. I'd like that. It will allow me the chance to tell you about my father, too.'

'Don't tell me he's still bothering you?'

Her cheery features suggested quite the opposite.

'Oh, he has his own issues to deal with at the moment. He was arrested by the Flying Squad in London today.'

It seemed like everyone and their dog was being caught by the police today.

'Arrested? How do you know this, Devina?'Georgia asked.

'Simple. I'm the one who provided them with the proof of all his illegal business dealings.'

212

17

Our scheme to rescue Bart Travis from his confinement failed. It shouldn't have, but it did. Possibly it was my fault, but even I could never see the future through those Elsewhen windows, only the past. Today, whatever skills I had to right the wrongs of the kidnappers didn't come to the rescue.

I hit my solid wooden table with my closed fist, instantly regretting my reactions as the pain surged up my arm. Devina stepped back, surprised by the extent of my frustration. At least Amber was asleep in bed and, sleeping as soundly as she did, wouldn't be awoken.

'I'm assuming that noise was you thumping something and not someone, Cindy.' Warren was on speaker phone and had rung after we'd been drinking.

Devina was fully conversant with all of the events of the past few days including our plan to trick Hannah.

Warren continued to explain what had, or more precisely, hadn't happened.

'Bart and his captors weren't at the location, but they had been. The burner phone was there, wiped clean, naturally, then destroyed. The room where the proof-of-life photographs were taken was there, along with signs that Bart was a prisoner there all week; food, empty takeaway packets, towels. Bleach everywhere to destroy DNA.

'They'd scarpered minutes before our blokes arrived. Hannah didn't warn them but they guessed we were coming. Maybe we should have been more low-key.

'Some locals put video of the arrest on Facebook or one of the gang may have seen her being led away in cuffs while they were shopping. Who knows? All I'm certain of is that poem by the Welsh bloke, Robbie Burns, sums today up. 'The best-laid schemes of cops an' women gang aft agley'.'

'He was Scottish,' I said without emotion.

'Whatever. We've caught two of the reprobates, Cindy. Small mercies.'

'So what now? I assume you and Dad have contingencies?'

'We pay the ransom as agreed and hope that we get lucky. I'm not going into operational procedures over the phone but his family have the money and the exchange is scheduled for two tomorrow.

'We have to believe that Bart will be released but this gang's track record is pretty bad so far. Quite frankly, love, we're out of options. We don't want them getting away scot-free but the possibility of them riding off into the sunset with two million quid is very real.' He sighed. I could hear the tiredness in his voice.

'How can they? We have their names, Thaddeus Giffen and that evil Shania. Maybe others. Can't you force Keith to disclose their getaway plans?'

'I'm not green enough to believe that they can't leave Britain, especially having that much cash. All Ports Warnings are great for major airports and ferry terminals, even Eurostar. Not much cop for a private plane or chopper. Even a yacht.

'If I were them, I'd lie low for a while before hightailing it. You were besties with Shania for a decade. Surely you . . . ?'

'Warren, she was sleeping with Jimmy for most of it and bunny-brained me never suspected.'

'Anyway. Just thought I'd bring you up to date. Got to go now. Coming up to ten. Another briefing with your father and the rest of the team and then a few hours' kip. Who'd be a copper's wife?'

Whether it was a throwaway statement or a typical Warren proposal, I wasn't sure. Two answers came to mind: 'I would' or 'Not me'. I opted for a third, one that kept him guessing about any future for us as a couple.

'Who indeed, Detective? Who indeed?'

* * *

Until now, Devina hadn't volunteered to elaborate on her bombshell announcement about shopping her dad to the authorities. I didn't push it. Reading between the lines, her family life had been one of oppressive control, at least by her father.

I was fully aware that, despite moving to another country and being immersed in another culture, many immigrants brought their baggage.

Warren had told me years ago at school a story from his parents and their courtship. He didn't do it to shock or say how weird Aussies were. Just that they simply thought differently.

'My Aussie grandparents were newlyweds in the early Seventies. They loved to go watch movies at the Drive-In theatres. You know, where you sit in your car with a speaker hooked over the window and watch the movie on a huge screen alongside hundreds of other cars in rows.

'They'd take a glass flagon of Sauterne, a Sarah Lee cheesecake and two straws. Gramps never drank much, not enough to put him over any limit, but it was the experience.

'Every time I have a glass of wine, even the last week back here in England, I'm tempted to ask for a straw. Perhaps one day, I will . . . for my grandad.'

It proved a point. Aussies, like most people living as aliens in Britain, wanted to keep their identity.

Relaxing with glasses of wine in our hands, Devina and I settled down to talk. On this occasion, Devina chose to take the lead. She was ready to engage and, hard as it had been for her, she decided to trust a friend with her traumatic story. That friend was me.

Unlike mine, her father wasn't a kind man. Moreover, he was involved in many enterprises that were shady.

Discovering that his daughter had impressive skills with numbers and accounting, even as a girl barely twelve, he exploited those talents effectively to massage the books in order to conceal his criminal enterprises. Devina was proficient with IT, too.

As she matured, she tried to rebel against his oppressive attitude until, a year earlier, she ran away, secretly supported by her kinder uncle. She'd taken records with her, threatening to expose her dad's nefarious and quite illegal actions should he ever follow her.

Last night, he had. Having learned so much away from his influence, she called his bluff. Those records, the ones that implicated him in various criminal enterprises, were currently in the hands of London police.

According to them, he'd been arrested earlier this afternoon. That was the phone call she was on when she came into The Love Affair.

'How do you feel? About doing that to your flesh and blood?' I asked, hugging her in support.

'Strangely elated. A huge weight has gone from my shoulders. He was never a caring father. My uncle, Hari, has always been more of a dad to me.'

With her brilliant mind, Devina was destined for great things in whatever field she chose. At present, she wished to avoid anything to do with economics, yet that might alter. Her father's exploitation of those talents had soured her of those fields.

As if to prove her point, she requested me to say two five-digit numbers at random which she multiplied mentally in five seconds. She was a prodigy. Even on my phone, it took me much longer to achieve the same answer.

'But my father now has his comeuppance and me, my revenge.'

I examined my friend with her ebony hair and flawless dusky skin. Her elfin features radiated nothing sinister at all.

'Revenge? That's not what I believed you're capable of, Devina. You've always been so reserved and genteel.'

'We all have our dark side, Cindy. Especially those who believed that they've been wronged. You and Shania. I hate her for what she's done to your life but you've shown me how to rise above the anger that eats away at your very soul.

'What you have achieved in your search for this lad who was taken, is commendable. It is that strength that convinced me not to allow myself to be intimidated by my past any more.'

I took a sip of my glass of Shiraz, leaning back in my chair to consider her sage words. In this season of goodwill, how magnanimous were Keith and Hannah feeling towards me, right at this instant?

Doubtless they blamed me for their incarceration although they were the criminals.

The trouble was, they weren't the only ones plotting against me. I was too over-confident to foresee what was heading my way.

18

Amber was very excited as she opened another Advent calendar door. Christmas was coming. The joys of her childhood certainly lightened my life.

'Eight more sleeps, Mummy.'

As we walked briskly through Hesketh Park, I wondered if more Elsewhens were lying in wait, ready to pounce upon me. Not today, it seemed. I'd avoided this gorgeous park all week since Monday, choosing to skirt the popular recreational area by using the surrounding streets.

I had such a rich connection to this place and it to me. So many comforting memories not forgetting that special first kiss. Since our encounter with Warren with the noisy cacophony of ducks, we'd had a hectic, exciting and sometimes scary week.

My Aussie and me were friends again. His grandparents and my family were talking to one another as well, welcoming

Amber into their fold.

Surprisingly, we were one big, happy, extended family as the planned Christmas dinner was scheduled to be a combined one at Colin and Brenda's larger home with everybody mucking in together. Georgia and Mike were invited and, at my request, Devina, too. Otherwise, she'd be alone.

The Brussels sprouts would be dutifully peeled with that little Christmas cross cut into them. As per tradition, they'd be eaten gleefully even though no-one would entertain them on a plate any other day of the year.

Mum's speciality was sweet glazed carrots, Dad's brandy butter for afters with the pud, and Georgia's a trifle. According to her, trifles consumed on Christmas Day had no calories at all.

As for my assigned task, it was far less ambitious. Given my questionable cooking skills that often caused the smoke alarm to scream in torment, my task was, under Amber's supervision, to provide and open packets of nibbles.

However, Devina deigned to accept my offer to help beforehand with making traditional Christmas snacks of Kulkuls and Achappam cookies.

As for Hannah, no invite for her. I'd ripped up the Christmas card that I'd written for her, deciding that the best she deserved for her devious actions, whilst in a cell on Christmas Day, was a stale mince pie that had been dropped on the floor.

But enough about Hannah. My thoughts turned to happier times ahead.

Yep. The good old days of a double festive celebration were back. All in all, it promised to be a Grand Day In. The final item I needed to buy was fresh mistletoe for Warren and me to test out, just like old times.

I peered at the skeletal trees above to see if there was mistletoe there. Meanwhile, Amber's eyes were searching the ground.

'Look, Mummy. A pine cone. It's all open.'

I showed her the pine seed, one of

which was inside. When I released it, the oval seed whirled around and around like a helicopter as it floated to the ground. The slow motion of its descent triggered changes around us.

Time stood still, the pine seed ceasing to spin and hovering motionless as though an invisible hand were holding it in mid-air. We stood amazed, as that mystical aura again enclosed us in a cocoon of loving warmth.

'What's happening, Mummy?' Amber asked, sensing the same as me.

'I'm not sure, love. But it's nothing to be afraid of. The park . . . I believe it's sharing a special Christmas gift with us because we love being here.'

'Oh, yes, Mummy. The air . . . it kissed my cheek. So soft.'

Although warmer, the air felt crisper, the lake waters sparkled like diamonds in the sunshine. Most noticeably, the dull hues of wintertime were as vibrant as on the brightest summer day.

On impulse, I knelt to scoop leaf litter in my gloved hand, lifting it to my face.

The rich aroma of cinnamon and sweet treacle rather than musty decay took me to a dream like world of euphoria for one ecstatic moment.

As time slowly resumed, squirrels appeared, scampering around at a time when they should be hibernating. It was a few days until the winter solstice.

Was this a reward for my helping to mitigate the murder of William Lockstone — a sort of thank you for trying to undo the errors of the past in part caused by me?

No answer came. Nevertheless, the memories of his death were avenged in some ethereal way. Whilst the squirrels cavorted playfully for Amber's amusement, my elation was now tinged with another aura, one more sinister. My role in this sorry tale of multiple lives in jeopardy both in the past and at the present wasn't yet over. Gusts of wintry winds resumed all around, teasing the few remaining leaves above to pirouette in a final dance of their short lives.

'Did you hear that, Mummy? The

wind whispering, 'Beware'? What does it mean?'

I bent to kiss Amber's rosy cheeks.

'It's reminding us to hurry up, pumpkin. Otherwise, Aunty Georgia will be cross with Mummy for being late again.'

We resumed our journey as the squirrels were long returned to their sanctuaries. I gritted my teeth. Beware of whom . . . or what? Enigmatic messages from the supernatural should have health warnings (or at least a hint to help people decipher their premonitions).

As we exited the natural wonderland on to Park Crescent, I stole a glance back, expecting who knew what. A blast of Arctic air caught me unawares. I overbalanced, acutely aware that if I fell, I'd drag Amber with me.

Ahead of us was a pool of water extending on to the road from the gutter. Reflected houses beckoned me to stumble in but I caught hold of a triangular give-way sign, stopping our fall. Amber's cone tumbled into the mirrored puddle, shattering the reflection as water splashed and ripples spread out.

Carefully, so as not to wet her feet or hands, she retrieved it to shake it dry. I stared down as the image coalesced once more. In that instant, before the cone hit though, I'd witnessed an omen.

Warren was looking up at me from the water. He wasn't there, of course, but a phantom of him was, staring back at me, his face contorted in horror.

* * *

Dad was at home when we arrived. He was extremely grumpy.

'Bart Travis is fine and reunited with his family. He's in hospital for observation but they're with him. Mind you, they're two million pounds poorer but that was their choice. Tell you what, I've half a mind to arrest them for letting the kidnappers get away.'

'I don't understand. Wasn't the hand-over set for this afternoon?'

He swigged a cup of black coffee, barely avoiding splashing it everywhere when he banged it on the table after half-emptying it.

'We were all set to trace the money. Electronic trackers in the middle of the wads of cash, drone surveillance at the drop-off location . . . all for nothing.

'Instead, the Travis family sneaked out at four this morning. They did it all direct with the kidnappers on a smuggled-in untraceable phone. Fooled us all, the Family Liason Officer, the guys monitoring their landline and mobiles. Made us look like right numpties.'

I appreciated his frustration but I understood why Bart's parents had done it. They wanted their son back in one piece and didn't trust the police not to jeopardise his life.

On the plus side, he was safe and that was important. Catching the criminals at this point was close to impossible. That was, unless Bart offered some inklings as to who they were and their escape route.

Dad was intending to collect Warren and then interview Bart at his bedside. He wasn't optimistic about learning a

229

thing. Whether by chance or design, the criminal crew had wrong-footed his investigative team. Dad's officers had been complacent, expecting to be one step ahead.

'We already know that he was drugged and blindfolded most of the time, too groggy to be aware of his surroundings. All he could offer at his initial debrief was one woman, two men.'

I suggested that coffee was the last thing Dad needed in his agitated state. Didn't Mum mention blood pressure fears a few weeks ago?

Although I sensed that he was ready to say, 'Mind your own business', he smiled wanly and agreed.

'Tell you one thing, Cindy. If you think that I'm angry, you should have heard Warren. Those Aussies know more swear words than I've ever heard and your boy-friend wasn't afraid to use them.'

'He's not my boyfriend.' My simple statement wasn't said with as much con-viction as it was a few days earlier.

Dad chuckled.

'You reckon? Want to reconsider that, Cindy?'

I blushed.

'OK, he is, but don't tell him yet. I'm trying to keep him guessing for a little while longer. A woman my age can't be seen to fall head over heels in love with the first gorgeous Aussie who comes along.'

Mum walked into the room, holding Amber's hand.

'We heard all about your jealousy of Kaitlyn, Cindy. I'm glad that he prefers you. We always wondered if he was the man for you. Looks like we were right, even though there was a big detour on the way.'

Dad grabbed his overcoat and gloves.

'May I offer you a lift to your shop, Cindy?'

'Yes, please. And thanks so much, Mum, for looking after Amber. What are you doing today?'

'We're going to play some board games, practise our alphabet and make paper decorations with tissue paper. Oh, and cooking of course.

'Warren gave me a recipe for lamingtons. They're a type of Aussie cake.'

Amber tugged on her sleeve, appearing concerned. My mind-reading mother reassured her.

'No. We won't be using real lambs, precious.'

That brought relief and smiles all around.

★ ★ ★

On our drive past the police station and down Lord Street with its myriad festive lights, my father was pleased to share his impressions of Warren.

'He's smart and dedicated, Cindy. Must admit it's taking us a while to get to grips with that accent of his. That's quite a confession considering we have people from Kirkby on the team.

'He mentioned, just in passing, mind you, that this year-long secondment from the New South Wales Police Force could be extended, maybe even permanent.

'I thought you had a right to know. In case things get serious, like.'

'I appreciate that news. Although there's the possibility that Amber and I might be asked to return with him in a year, I'm reluctant to do that.

'There's the shop and you and Mum and so many other things that I love about Southport. It sounds mad, but Australia isn't on my 'to-do' list.

'Family is so important to me. I learnt that when I left you to go with Jimmy. Thankfully, Warren's not Jimmy but the principle is the same. Southport's in my blood, Elsewhens and all.'

★ ★ ★

Devina proved herself invaluable that busy Sunday. She was effusively friendly, competent and everything we dreamed of in a work colleague. What was better was her suggestions gleaned from her year-long stint at Harrod's. In those rare moments when we weren't busy, she indicated improvement with traffic flow and eye-level product placement.

Moreover, she wanted nothing in return save the possibility to be employed full-time until university resumed, then part-time thereafter.

Georgia accepted her verbal job application late in the day. Other items such as tax and NI details would be sorted tomorrow.

Warren rang me mid-afternoon with an update on Bart. Our one-time schoolmate was unable to provide any further insights into the identities of his captors or the locations in which he was imprisoned.

For their part, his parents were quite defensive of their actions, adamant that they did what was best for Bart's safe release. That their disregard for the police plans might encourage more kidnappings was a factor they'd not considered. It was a sobering reality for them.

I didn't mention my latest otherworldly experience in Hesketh Park, nor the spectral voice whispering, 'Beware'. In a phone conversation, it would put a dampener on any further chatting.

That was the last thing that I desired. I'd come to revel in the smooth, sultry tone of his voice. Instead, I suggested dinner at mine. He accepted on the condition that he cooked. My reputation preceded me.

My plan was to confess, once and for all, that I did love him. That was quite a step for me. My baggage might cause issues for our future relationship but one thing I'd learned over these past days was 'what ifs' were just that. It was time to take a chance on real love.

When Mum phoned with her daily progress report on Amber, she listened patiently to my declaration, saying that it was about time I realised that he was the one for me.

I was surprised. She'd seen our bond way back in school, as had Dad and Georgia. It appeared the single person not to realise it was me.

Some of that was down to Shania's manipulations but I couldn't blame her entirely. I was shallow and Warren wasn't my idea of a perfect tall, dark, handsome boyfriend.

'Why not let Amber have another sleepover, love? Dad will relish another chance to play with his choo-choos and unwind and I'm sure you'd prefer some privacy.'

The vision of me and Warren together elicited sensations which I hadn't experienced, at least not for many years. My relationship with Jimmy was infatuation at first, degrading to acceptance that this was all life offered someone as mediocre as me. Jimmy achieved that slowly, yet inexorably and finally completely.

By contrast, Warren reawakened that joy and excited passion of my youth. It was time to experience real love in its angelic glory. I prayed that my dreams of what might be would not disappoint me yet again.

19

Devina and I decided to walk home. We reached The Bold Hotel about halfway back to our respective apartments. Even here, the sounds of muted Christmas carols played through street speakers, filled the air with a sense of anticipation for the coming holidays. Devina paused, put a hand to her forehead and apologised.

'Goodness. Just remembered I need some spices and rice flour. I'll nip back to the World Food shop. Won't be a tick.'

I clasped my arms around my body, shivering a little despite my warm coat.

My breath formed tiny clouds in front of my face. Even though I suggested the shop at the service station, the other side of the roundabout, Devina shook her pretty head.

'No way will they have what I need.'

'Fair enough. I'll wait here, kiddo. Don't be long. Otherwise, there'll be another Christmas decoration . . . Me, frozen solid.'

I cast my eye over the façade of the famous hotel. The recent renovations had done it proud. Having been associated with Red Rum in his championship days, The Bold sported a striking statue of him on the roof of the main entranceway.

Because it was Sunday evening, there were few people outside on the footpath although quite a crowd of diners were visible through the windows.

I turned, watching Devina some hundred yards off before shivering from my lack of movement. I stamped my feet to ward off the cold

'Silent Night' was being sung, relaxing me with its lullaby music. It was beautiful, reminding me of Christmases long gone. Noddy Holder and Wham! had their place in the weeks — sorry, months — leading up to Our Lord's birthday celebrations, but they never replaced traditional carols in my mind.

I fidgeted, stamping my feet as I

soaked up the magnificent fairy light atmosphere, too; the white lights that adorned the trees all year round and the seasonal conical artificial trees with their sparkling rainbow spirals in the roundabout centre.

One thing was certain about my home town; Southport loved its illuminations.

Periodically, I checked for my friend's return. What was keeping her?

A van pulled up behind me, its presence dimly registering as it passed slowly before stopping.

If it had been the usual white, I may have thought nothing of it but it was midnight black. I stared back down Lord Street again, waiting impatiently.

At last she appeared, rather flustered. A group of other customers who were walking in the other direction must have delayed her at the single till.

A tap on my right shoulder startled me. I'd not heard anybody approaching from behind. As I moved, I noticed the black van, side door ajar.

That one-word warning, 'Beware',

came to mind. The adrenalin coursed through my blood to every part of my body — fight or flight.

Eyeing up the brutish man standing by a more slightly built woman, I had no chance of either.

'Long time no see, Lucy-Lou,' the woman sneered.

'Not long enough, Miss Piggy.' Poking fun at her Muppet like habit of brushing her hair seductively felt hollow but the flash of anger at the insult showed me that this older Cindy wasn't ready to capitulate at the first threat.

Nevertheless, feeling a frisson of fear, I weighed up my options. From behind, I heard footsteps, running towards me.

Devina was coming. My friend called my name hysterically.

For one anxious moment, I wondered if Devina had set me up, a second traitor posing as a friend. But no, her cries were for others to join her in protecting me.

Sadly, no-one else was around and I doubted that drivers in cars would realise my peril. I tensed as a sharp item nicked my half-exposed neck.

'Just to relax you, Lucy-Lou. Or should I call you, Sleeping Ugly? Nighty night.' I began to feel unsteady, my legs like jelly. My muscles wouldn't respond.

As I slumped, the hulkish brute grabbed me, half-carrying me to the van.

I stared through blurring vision as Devina was joined by four men, exiting The Bold. Thankfully, they understood my dilemma.

Just as my eyes closed Devina lifted her phone to take photos.

She'd realised that she and the men wouldn't reach me in time and was snapping the van and number plate.

Inside the van, I felt hard metal as I landed heavily. The door slammed shut and the idling motor surged forward, cutting a car off, by the sound of a horn behind us.

I'd been abducted, just like Bart had a week earlier. And just like Bart, I was helpless to save myself.

20

I'd never been a morning person and today was no exception. The added effect of whatever knock-out injection Shania had given me didn't help one iota.

The room was in almost complete darkness a part from alight to my left. Certainly not daylight, not even the pitiful excuse of a British winter.

I tried to focus on my watch as I raised my arm nearer to my eye. Every part of my body protested, reminding me of teenage days and my first hangover, awakening in the bath.

The fun watch that I wore for Amber's amusement and education slowly became clear. Mickey's two hands were pointing straight up on the watch. Did that mean he was surrendering to some unseen enemy? No, it meant it was noon and Lucinda Powers was in deep trouble.

'Is that you sitting by my bedside,

Shania? Same stinky pound shop perfume. Or is that your new boyfriend I smell?'

I was on a bed, still clothed but constrained. My fingers touched plastic. It crinkled. A sleeping bag? Surely not. I forced myself to focus as I turned my head. Shania's smirking face stared back at me.

'Now, now, Sleeping Ugly. Is that any way to address the person holding you prisoner in a place no-one, not even that colonial clown copper of yours, can find you?'

She walked around the bed to turn the battery-powered light up to full. The walls shone back in places. It took me a moment to realise that it was damp literally running down the surfaces from leaks in the roof above.

I never used to insult her, not at school when she gave me useless fashion tips and advice on boys and not as my best friend when I was married whilst she secretly shared his bed.

However, one aspect of Shania

Featherley's psyche that I noticed time and again, was her hatred at being belittled. Underneath her brass and bravado, Shania was riddled with confidence issues same as me.

The difference was her façade of being an alpha girl. Breaking through that was my sole chance to undermine whatever plan she had for me now.

'Wow. I'm very impressed with your place, Miss Piggy. Love the décor. Pinterest must be clamouring to do a photo shoot for their more discerning clients.'

Her eyes blazed with anger as she stood over me menacingly.

'It's my grand-aunt's house. Abandoned for years but perfect for hiding our precious kidnap victims in. We were forced to bring Bart here when our other hidey-hole was compromised by silly Hannah. Good thing I saw her being arrested. It gave me and Thaddeus a chance to move him here before the coppers caught us.'

Well done, Shania. You've told me a lot, probably more than you intended.

If I have a chance of escaping, I need information and to have her on the back foot.

The roof line of my soggy prison room indicated we were in the attic. No window. I racked my brains to recall conversations and places visited. Yes. I'd been here as a teenager. It was on a suburban road of sorts, with other properties well spread out. In retrospect, I recalled disputes about who the legal owner was. Certainly not my captor.

Shania boasted when we were inside as kids that it had hidden rooms with secret access. It was evident that Shania's criminal nature ran in the family as her ancestors probably hid other people or contraband here.

A scratching noise caused us both to scan the room. A mouse scurried across alongside the skirting board to a hole in the rotting wood. The stench of dampness, mingled with Shania's perfume, was quite overpowering.

Matilda Mouse, I thought. My mind drifted to Amber's Christmas book.

'Matilda Mouse and the Gingerbread House". The diminutive rodent was so proud of her home in the sunshine, made of all things sweet.

If she was feeling peckish her miraculous residence tempted her with a sweet for eating, then replaced it by magic. But one day, the rains came, soaking her gingerbread walls until they easily broke into small pieces causing the house to sag, ready to collapse in ruins.

If it weren't for Santa Claus coming to the rescue, with his reindeer, Matilda would have been homeless. The reindeer flew high into the skies and politely asked the rain to stop.

Then Santa gave Mr Sun a sun hat as a present. Mr Sun was so pleased he shone and shone, drying out the gingerbread and making the house as good as new.

Amber loved that story. I felt comfort in knowing that she was being cared for by Mum and Dad. With an effort, I pushed missing her to one side. Sitting up, I concentrated on my present predicament.

'Warren and my father will find me, Shania. Count on it.'

She was more composed again.

'Doubt it, Cindy. We swapped vans soon after taking you. Just in case anyone clocked the number plate. Left your phone in the old van, too. No-one apart from the three of us has a clue where you're being held.

'Even if the cops do search the house, they'll never find this room or the secret panel to its stairs.'

I felt despondent at that news but refused to show it.

'So why snatch me off the street? You have your two million already and my family don't have that sort of cash.'

'Two reasons. I've demanded the cash from your trust fund. Half a million twelve years ago when you mentioned it to me. I figure seven hundred thousand today. It's always been about getting your money, you idiot.

'Jimmy and me were going to split it after you reached twenty-eight and became entitled to it but with the divorce, I needed another way. Assisting Thaddeus to abduct that Travis guy helped but really, I want what's mine.'

'It's never been yours, you fool.'

I touched a nerve. She lost it immediately, yelling at me.

'It's mine, Cindy. Mine. I earned every single pound. Being your best friend all those years, listening to your whiny voice, fawning over you, getting rid of Warren with those posters that set him up as the person responsible.

'Then pretending that I was there for you to cry your eyes out. Even lining you up with Jimmy for you to fall in love with. Plus I had to keep him sweet otherwise he would have taken all your trust fund for himself.

'So much effort and for what? Nothing. It's . . . it's so unfair.' She began to cry. I didn't commiserate one bit.

Finally, she stopped feeling sorry for herself long enough for me to ask, 'Are you and Jimmy finished, then?'

'Finished? Finished! You bet we're

finished. I don't know how you put up with that piece of garbage but, once his usefulness to me was over, so was he.'

Maybe it was the sadness in her voice that alerted me to inquire about my former husband.

'You didn't kill him, did you?'

'Kill him? Of course not. I'm not that evil a woman, Cindy.'

'Yet here we are, Shania. You kidnapping me and demanding money with menaces. That sounds pretty darn evil to me.'

'Yeah. I can see that argument but there are different degrees of evil. None of our gang are murderers. Not me, Keith, Hannah or Timmy. Thaddeus was the one who killed that bloke ten years ago, that diabetic chap.'

Well, that was an interesting statement.

'But Keith confessed.'

'Thaddeus is a master manipulator. Keith is vulnerable. He's been lied to by Thaddeus for his entire life.

'Sure, old Thad loves Keith and

indulges him with his butterflies but it was Thaddeus who misread what to do if a person's in a diabetic coma. Keith gave that unfortunate lad the sugar on his father's instructions. Need I say more?'

It made sense. Keith might have been a bully to Warren but it was his way of being lashing out after his mistreatment.

Yet I was surprised by this conversation. Shania was sharing her feelings with me. Our friendship had been a sham on her part yet the saddest fact was that I was her only close friend. She still felt as if she might exchange confidences.

In her way, she was as screwed up as Keith, never allowing herself to be genuine with anyone — me, Jimmy or herself.

Realising that, perhaps, she stood and went to a relatively dry wall in her house of horrors. She opened a wooden door that, like the exit door to the stairs, blended imperceptibly into the wood panelling.

'You've a bathroom in here and change of clothes, underwear, too. I remember your sizes from when we went shopping.

I chose stuff your like, plain but pretty. A warm jumper too.

'There's running water for the shower connected to a bottle-gas fuelled instant hot water system. I'm not the monster you believe I am, Cindy.'

'Thanks. I never thought you were a monster, Shania. You can still let me go.'

'Don't think so. I'll let you get cleaned up. There's drinks in that cupboard over there, cold water and juice and biscuits. Also, a gas camping stove if you fancy a cuppa or coffee.

'Tom's bringing some hot food later when it's dark. I've already contacted your family with my ransom demands. Your trust fund. All of it. I'm leaving now. The door is solid and locked so don't think about trying to escape. I'm sorry it had to end like this but I need that money for a fresh start overseas.'

'What about if I attacked you to get the door key?'

'No chance, love. That injection I gave you might feel like it's worn off but the minute you move you'll see. Head spinning, weak legs and muscles. Best not to try anything too strenuous.'

I tested her assertion by trying to stand. She was correct. I had no chance in a fight. Even walking to the very welcome bathroom was going to be an effort.

Shania left me to my devices as she unlocked the exit door.

'See you later, old friend.' Her sad voice prompted me to be quiet rather than yell vindictive words back. Whoever said that the villain is the hero in their own story was right. She wasn't going to change her mind.

That meant one thing. I had to call on all of my strength to escape from this hell hole and be with my darling daughter again.

21

Refreshed and warmed by the shower, I dressed quickly. Considerately, Shania had provided a mirror, toiletries and a brush. Unlike the bedroom, the bathroom was cleaned, tiled throughout and without any damp issues.

It was incongruous in this house of horrors yet I accepted that Shania's mind was not logical.

Perhaps it was her concession to her captives or maybe she'd done it up for herself as a DIY project. She always fancied herself as a designer. I was able to stand and move more freely as the effects of the injection dissipated.

I'd showered with the help of two battery lamps, again there being no window. Back in the bedroom, I set about making a hot drink and devouring a sandwich which was labelled as part of a Meal Deal. I'd need my strength for whatever lay ahead.

The paraffin fumes concerned me and potential carbon monoxide from the old heater. It served a purpose but I needed air circulation from outside, even if the room became colder as a result.

The mouse appeared again, scavenging for food. I thought of that gingerbread house her fictional counterpart called home. This place was clad in rotting timbers — at least the top part.

I returned to the bathroom searching for a broomstick or some other long strong object. A metal towel rail on the wall was the best I found. Pulling it gently, I felt the rawl plugs fixed into the tiles and wall give a little. Another tug and one bracket came loose allowing me to remove the yard-long chrome rail from the supports.

Elated, I returned to the bedroom and gingerly lifted a corner of the heavy plastic tarpaulin strung across what was logically covering the outside wall of the house.

The stench of released damp and decaying wood forced me back, gagging.

The cover must have been holding the smell back from the main part of the room.

Holding my breath, I poked my stick at the wall. It went straight through the interior wall, dislodging parts of it that fell to the wet floor with more of a squish than a clatter. Enlarging the hole with more pokes revealed the outside weatherboard horizontal cladding.

The planks were clearly visible, one hanging loose at an angle where either the wood around the nail had rotted or the nails had rusted through. Fresh air never smelt as sweet. Although it was freezing cold, there was no wind, therefore, with the tarp back in place, Shania wouldn't suspect the hole I'd made.

Outside there was a powder blue sky and the tops of trees. My watch said two forty. Sunset was around ten to four. Could I make a hole large enough to crawl through to freedom? Probably. But then what? I was thirty feet up; two storeys with ten-foot ceilings, then bearers and floors before the attic level.

My tomboy days of climbing trees

were long behind me. The outside structure, downpipes, guttering and so on were unstable and, given the nature of the weather, wet and icy.

My chances of surviving a fall from this height were zero to minus ten.

I didn't have a Plan B. Gently testing the other wooden panels on the outside, I found many were as rotten as the one already dislodged. I hesitated to push them open in case Shania noticed when she returned.

Instead, I withdrew, rearranged the heavy tarpaulin to cover my actions and accepted that gentle wafts of fresh air and a cooler room were the best I could achieve at this time.

Preparing a second hot drink, I sat on the surprisingly clean bed to consider my dire straits. Frankly, I had no idea if my trust fund was accessible before my twenty-eighth birthday.

Georgia had one, too, although Shania didn't appear to realise that. Small mercies. When the solicitor announced our legacy soon after our paternal grandmother passed, maybe I should have quizzed him about the present predicament.

'Excuse me, sir, but can you tell me if, on the slim chance that my deranged ex-best friend kidnaps me and demands the money from my trust fund two years early, can she have it?'

Shania was desperate and clutching at straws. The same with Thaddeus who, according to Shania, planned a prisoner exchange, me for his son Keith. They both had unrealistic expectations of my bargaining value.

What might happen if they didn't get their way? Nothing good for me, I suspected. My single chance was being found by the police who were out searching for me.

A few minutes later, I heard footsteps on the stairs followed by a rapid unlocking of the door. Shania appeared, agitated. For a split second, I hesitated then made a move to take her down. She stepped aside nimbly, plunging another needle into the arm she caught hold of as I stumbled forward. It hurt.

This time the effect was instantaneous. I was paralysed before I crashed to the floor. I didn't pass out, though. I heard Shania's heavy breathing as she lay beside me as still as still could be.

My eyes were open but all I saw was the ceiling. Voices from down below became louder.

'Looks deserted,' one woman shouted from the grounds below.

'Well, it would. Check inside. Search every room on every floor.' Was that Warren directing people?

'Check the cellar if there's one. Any sign it's been used? Report back to me, by radio. Work in pairs, too. These people are dangerous.'

I tried to call out, only managing a murmur as my lips wouldn't move.

Shania, fearing detection, clamped her hand over my mouth, forcing me to breathe through my nose. I was already struggling as my diaphragm muscles were affected, the same as my legs and arms. Realising this, she released her hand.

More voices, from right underneath us, filtered up through the outside wall that I punctured. Shania was panicking now.

'How did they track you down? No-one knows about this house.'

With a start, I recalled that I did. I'd written about it in my diaries. Had my family read them?

Not that I was bothered if it saved my life.

My father's rich baritone carried up to me.

'Check out any signs of footprints outside in the mud, Kalowski.'

We heard officers moving methodically through the house. I assumed that the lower levels and staircases weren't as rotten as this part. On one occasion, voices were just on the other side of our wall.

'Nothing in the attic. Place is falling to bits up here. I can see daylight through the walls. Even the supports are rotted through.

'Looks like water pipes up here.

Strange. There's no header tank. Do you want me to check it out, guv? Floor looks solid.'

It was the water supply to the bathroom that I used. Whoever built this secret section didn't expect that a search would be this thorough.

I guessed that the policeman was standing on a ladder they'd brought and was peering around the open part of the attic next door to us. He'd be shining his torch around the access hole from the floor below.

I was sure that he'd discover the secret room if he explored the void. You might hide a room's existence and stairs from below and from outside but not from a closer examination. Why put a wall up to block off part of an attic?

My dad's voice cracked through the radio link.

'No, Jonesy. No point. Don't bother closing the trapdoor. Just get down. Maybe one of the others found something.'

Shania breathed a sigh of relief. All

I could do was cry, unable to move or scream for help. My one chance . . . gone.

They left soon after. Shania stood warily.

'That was close. Too close. But they won't be back. As for you, Cindy, that injection of that paralytic drug will wear off soon. Normally the docs would have you on breathing assistance but I checked the dosage with the internet. You should be fine.'

Great. Doctor internet. How could any person be so cavalier with dangerous drugs? As if feeling a touch of responsibility, she stayed until I was fully mobile, although very cold. I guessed my blood pressure was affected by her recklessness, too. It was pitch black outside when she left.

That allowed me to peek behind the tarp to the holes I'd made in the outside wall. An owl flying through the trees of the woods, hooted a greeting.

I sat back on the bed feeling totally desperate. My rescuers had arrived as I prayed they would. If only I could have grabbed their attention, leaning out of a makeshift window in the rickety structure this high up. Thank goodness that the roof beams were stronger than the framework for the boards on the outside.

I kept thinking about Matilda Mouse's gingerbread house for an inexplicable reason. Rotten from the rain, just like this. If I broke through the walls to the outside, what was the point? No-one was around to hear or see it. Also, I doubted that Shania and her muscle-bound friend would be too chuffed with my efforts.

As if in answer to my prayers, the room became lighter. It was from the outside. A searchlight? No. Approaching the pulled-backtarp, I stared out. Sunshine?

A voice. My dad's voice, again.

'. . . signs of footprints outside in the mud, Kalowski.'

He'd come back. Somehow he'd come back. But then why repeat those exact same words from earlier and how did it suddenly become daytime outside?

When the truth hit me, I rushed to rip the tarpaulin down from its anchor points on the ceiling and drag it to one side of the room.

Light from outside now shone through the numerous gaps in the outside wall, illuminating the room and giving me a flood of endorphins. I had a chance to be seen by those police down below but had to act quickly before my Elsewhen window vanished.

Pushing boards off with the towel rail was too slow. The Elsewhen was an unstable hole in time. I needed to make an impact and soon, destroying the wall in any way possible.

The bed? It was on rollers. If I gathered enough momentum . . . ? Angling the iron frame diagonally I garnered all of my strength and pushed it towards the hole-dotted wall. It was so heavy.

Slowly it began to move, gathering speed as I pushed with all my might. The floor splinters tore into my bare feet.

I yelled in pain and in an attempt to make myself heard above the conversations down below. Moving police cars probably drowned out any calls for help so this was my one chance.

The corner of the bed ripped through the interior wall like a knife through butter but met resistance with the more substantial wood on the exterior. I kept pushing. The walls and boards splintered and broke until the bed hung precariously, one-third now outside the building.

Anyone below would have heard the screaming timbers in their death throes and run from danger so I grunted and pushed one last time.

The bed tore through the rest of the wood and fell. The crash was deafening as it hit the brick path below. I held on to the jagged edge of the still-intact wall and leaned out precariously.

The bed was there, bent and useless with debris and fragments of wood and plaster scattered all around. No people, though. Just wreckage.

I'd failed. Worse still, clomping footsteps resounded on the hidden staircase leading to my secret prison. Shania? The Elsewhen was fading, night replacing day as reality returned to normal.

The key turned in the door lock and Shania burst in. One look at where the bed had been and then to the moonlit trees visible through a huge gap where the outside of her precious room once was and then to me. The wind howled into the room as I shivered in the near-freezing damp air.

Shadows from the dim battery-powered lamp gave us both a spectral appearance as we glared at one another.

There wasn't much I could say to cover up what I'd done in my escape attempt.

So instead I smiled weakly, bent my head and apologised.

'Ooops. So sorry, Shania. I broke your house. It was an accident. Honest.'

Any hopes that she, like Dad, might forgive me, were unlikely. Nevertheless, I was unprepared for what happened next.

Screaming abuse, Shania ran towards me and pushed me back towards the void and the thirty-foot fall through the air to the ground below.

22

They say that your life flashes before your eyes as you're about to die. I'm not sure who 'they' are but I was certainly about to die. Shania's temper and my precarious position thirty feet above a mangled metal-framed bed with jagged shards pointing up, pretty well ensured my fate.

Yet it wasn't my life I saw. Just Warren's face in that puddle near Hesketh Park staring up at me.

Desperately I gazed down to the last vestiges of the Elsewhen below. Warren was there, his face looking directly at mine. He'd seen me through the Elsewhen that had linked the afternoon search by the police to my night time drama, scant hours later, fighting for my life.

Shania was a mad woman, intent on pushing me from the remnants of the room. Gone was her desire for whatever ransom she might collect. Revenge was all that lay behind her maniacal eyes.

Just as she was about to begin her final assault, Warren burst into the room from the unlocked door to the stairs. He and two police officers grabbed Shania, pulling her back, restraining her flailing arms and legs as they handcuffed her.

Warren left them to grab my hand, pulling me back to the room and into his arms.

'Cutting it a bit too fine, mate,' I half-joked after I finished sobbing uncontrollably in relief.

He dabbed my cheeks with a tissue before kissing me tenderly on my fore-head, eyes, cheeks and finally lips. I responded passionately.

'Thank heavens you're all right,' my father said, entering the room. I broke from Warren's embrace to hug my father.

'Do you mind if we continue this in warmer surroundings?' I asked through chattering teeth. 'I wouldn't say no to a meal and a hot shower either.'

'Paramedics are downstairs. Hospital

first then debrief. You're safe now, love.'

'Thaddeus? And that chap who helped Shania snatch me?'

'Both in custody,' Dad replied, filling me with relief. Amber's fine, too, although we may have told her a little white lie about being poorly.'

As we began to leave, the mouse scurried across the floor to her gap in what was left of the skirting board.

'Bye, Matilda,' I said, waving farewell.

'Friend of yours?' Warren asked ushering me out the door.

'She planned my escape with the battering-ram bed, sort of. Shame about her home being wrecked, though.'

★ ★ ★

Hours later, in my parents' house, with Amber cuddled up on my left and Warren on my right, he explained to us all what happened in my absence.

As I guessed, Mum read my diary and realised the importance of my mention of the abandoned house Shania took me to as a girl. Detective work revealed the location of Shania's relative's house near Sniggerty Wood.

They found nothing in the afternoon search and were about to leave when Warren sensed a change from around the back of the house. Investigating, he was just in time to see me hanging out of the part-destroyed room on the other side of the Elsewhen.

'Why on earth, didn't you rescue me then? In the afternoon?'

'Devina explained it to us, Cindy. Cause and Effect. We had to wait until after you crashed your bed through the wall. Only then could we save you.'

I thought so hard my brain began to hurt again then I understood. Time-travel paradoxes were way beyond me but it was logical.

If the police force broke into the secret stairway and rooms in the afternoon when I was drugged, I wouldn't have awoken and broken the wall to tell Warren where I was at night.

If I never did that, then no-one would

guess where I was. Those four hours or so had to proceed uninterrupted but, in the meantime, plans were made by the later Warren to save me the moment after the earlier Warren saw me through the time window.

Warren's grandparents, who were listening to the revelations along with Devina, were struggling with the whole concept, too. Finally, Colin admitted that it happened and that was that. All the ransom money had been recovered and the criminals were in prison. Then he laughed.

'I feel sorry for you police, though. How are you going to explain these Else-when things in your reports and at the trials?'

Dad and Warren exchanged glances. Dad answered. 'We've been thinking about that. Best to keep certain aspects of Cindy's rescue between ourselves. Call it a Christmas miracle or whatever.'

'Too right,' Warren agreed. 'As that Scottish bloke, Bill Shakespeare, wrote, 'All's well that ends well'.'

Christmas Eve and Day arrived without any further dramas, thank goodness. Amber was spoilt with presents, including a very special one from Santa.

As a family, we attended the Christmas service at our local church before driving to Colin and Barbara's place. Once unloaded, the quantity of food was obscene but would do us for the next week or so.

I managed to prepare and cook some Paxo stuffing all by myself without causing any fires. Crackers were pulled, paper hats worn and cringeworthy jokes read out. It was absolutely the best Christmas ever.

Someone from Down Under (no names mentioned) had hung mistletoe in a dozen locations around the house. He insisted we try every one of them. By the last one, my lips needed lip balm but we agreed that the experience was well worth it.

After clearing up from our meal,

Amber, Warren and I chose to visit Hesketh Park, for old times' sake. It was our special place.

By the time we arrived the afternoon was almost done. Amber, being younger and more energetic than us, kept running off and returning, always clearly visible. The park was virtually deserted.

One time, she stopped and looked at something of interest across the lake, hidden from us by bushes and trees.

'What is it, pumpkin?'

'Those people over there. Why are they waving to me?'

'Perhaps they know you, Amber?' Warren suggested as they came into our view too.

Two adults stood watching us, all done up in their winter woollies. Three children were waving madly, a girl around ten and two younger ones, a girl about five and a boy barely three.

'I don't recognise them,' I said, puzzled.

'Well, strike me pink,' Warren declared using one of those unfathomable Aussie expressions of his.

'I recognise him — and her. You should, too, Cindy. You see the mother every day in the mirror,' Warren said, noting the resemblance before I did.

'Goodness me.' I hadn't realised we were staring through an Elsewhen, this time to the future.

'That's you, Warren. Looking a little follicly challenged too. And that older girl . . . That's you, Amber.'

'Me? But I'm here.'

'That's a grown-up you. See. She has your scarf and Koka Koala in her hand, just like you.'

Simultaneously, both Warrens began to take photos as the children on the other side of the Elsewhen unravelled a banner.

I waved, as did Amber.

'You realise this gives a whole new meaning to the word 'selfie',' Warren announced. By now, the banner was open, being held at waist level by everyone over the lake. 'Merry Christmas from 2029', it read.

We couldn't hear them, nor they us, but the message was there. My days of experiencing Elsewhens were not finished yet. As to other adventures, I'd just have to wait and see.

We stayed there for as long as the Elsewhen allowed, another eight minutes of love and joy being shared across the years.

'Talk about a very special present,' Warren announced as we made our way back to our families.

I laughed, hugging him and Amber to me as we walked.

'I wonder how they'll react when we show them the photos. Two other children in our family.'

Warren scrolled through the photos and video he'd taken then stopped without warning, giving me the phone.

'You may wish to revise that number, darling.'

I gasped as I zoomed in on the future me. I was pregnant.

'Might be twins?'

'Or triplets?' I added.

One thing was certain, though. Our family had many happy Christmases to come.